T0009597

Love in the Time of Time's Up

Love in the Time of Time's Up
Short Fiction Edited by Christine Sneed

Tortoise Books
Chicago, IL

FIRST EDITION, OCTOBER, 2022

"The Elevator," Copyright © 2022 Karen Bender; "In an Academic Grove," Copyright © 2022 May-lee Chai; "Dudes, in Theory," Copyright © 2022 Elizabeth Crane; "The Swamp in Her Voice," Copyright © 2022 Rebecca Entel; "Slut Lullabies," Copyright © 2022 Gina Frangello; "A Good Plan," Copyright © 2022 Joan Frank; "Lil," Copyright © 2022 Melissa Fraterrigo; "Sunshine," Copyright © 2022 Lynn Freed; "Preferences" and "We Wonder (Ode to Lisa Lisa)," Copyright © 2022 Amina Gautier; "Former Virgin," Copyright © 2022 Cris Mazza; "The Sacrament of Brett," Copyright © 2022 Roberta Montgomery; "Superman," Copyright © 2022 Victoria Patterson; "Comeback," Copyright © 2022 Jenny Shank; "Potpourri," Copyright © 2022 Christine Sneed; "How To Walk on Water," Copyright © 2022 Rachel Swearingen; "Something Transcendent at the Heart," Copyright © 2022 Alison Umminger

Anthology Copyright © 2022 by Tortoise Books

All rights reserved under International and Pan-American Copyright Convention
Published in the United States by Tortoise Books

www.tortoisebooks.com

ISBN-13: 978-1-948954-7-16

This book is a work of fiction. All characters, scenes and situations are either products of the author's imagination or are used fictitiously. Any resemblance to actual events or locales or persons, living or dead, is coincidental.

Cover Design by Gerald Brennan. Copyright ©2022 by Tortoise Books. Shutterstock image 1070080670 used with permission per standard Shutterstock license.

Tortoise Books Logo Copyright ©2022 by Tortoise Books. Original artwork by Rachele O'Hare.

Contents

Introduction

The Me Too and Time's Up movements gained propulsive momentum in the fall of 2017 after *New York Times'* reporters Jodi Kantor and Meghan Twohey published an incendiary article about Harvey Weinstein's decades' long history of paying hush money to women he had sexually assaulted. Soon after the Weinstein story broke, many other well known, powerful men were called out for similar misconduct.

The Weinstein allegations, like those against U.S. Gymnastics' team doctor Larry Nassar, continued to grow in number after the story broke, thus ushering in an unprecedented moment in Western history: the public figures and captains of industry who had arguably considered themselves above the law were now being called to account for past actions, ones that compromised many women's (and in some cases, men's) ability to perform their jobs or advance in their professions.

Les Moonves, Roger Ailes, Bill O'Reilly, Kevin Spacey, Bryan Singer, and Matt Lauer were among the powerful men who joined Harvey Weinstein and Larry Nassar in the town pillory, to name only a few who were accused of serial sexually inappropriate behavior, many of their victims their colleagues and subordinates.

Me Too- and Time's Up-related incidents continue to fuel heated conversations on social media, and related stories still appear in the national and international news, particularly those linked to Hollywood and broadcast journalism, and there is no indication that these discussions, ostensibly reboots and offshoots of the feminist movement, will disappear anytime soon.

Enter *Love in the Time of Time's Up: A Short Fiction Anthology,* which features short stories addressing the subjects of

Me Too and Time's Up from sixteen different points of view—each short story written by an accomplished author, each author a woman.

The success of Kristen Roupenian's *New Yorker* short story "Cat Person" in December 2017 has made apparent—all debates aside regarding the popularity of fiction versus nonfiction—that people love a good short story, perhaps especially when sex, questionable behavior, and vulnerability figure into the narrative. According to *New Yorker* fiction editor Deborah Treisman, "Cat Person" found a readership far beyond what is habitual for the magazine's short stories—it went unexpectedly viral.

One of fiction's great rewards is that it allows writers to examine and explore controversy, along with the contradictory aspects of the human heart, therefore offering writers and readers alike the freedom to imagine and reimagine events, ideally enlarging the personal and transforming it into the universal, as Roupenian did with "Cat Person." (In July 2021, incidentally, Roupenian was in the news again for having borrowed many of the story's details from an actual couple in Ann Arbor, Michigan, where the author went to graduate school. The woman who was the basis of the main character in "Cat Person," Alexis Nowicki, not surprisingly, was upset when she realized her relationship with an older man had been fictionalized without her permission and in a manner that did not hold true to her experience of it. Roupenian responded with contrition, as a much-shared article in *Slate* by Nowicki chronicled.)

When assembling the stories in this anthology, I was particularly interested in work that subverted some of the traditional masculine and feminine character attributes, and rather than blaming men categorically for bad behavior, I was interested in exploring a range of perspectives on sexual power and its abuses and was also hoping to include at least one or two stories with comic elements, and in that respect, Elizabeth Crane's story "Dudes, in Theory" is what I'd call a masterly portrayal of the complicated social behavior both sexes are prey to. This is one of the funniest, and ultimately, most tender and poignant stories I've read in a long time.

Roberta Montgomery's story, "The Sacrament of Brett," although topically different from Crane's "Dudes, in Theory," similarly struck me as refreshingly risk-taking. In "Sacrament," the author has imagined a series of diary entries and confessional sessions between Brett Kavanaugh and his priest, beginning in the 1980s. Montgomery is so adept at plumbing both the moral confusion and chilling self-righteousness of one of the most controversial Supreme Court justices ever to be confirmed.

Reading through each of the stories in this volume, I was both thrilled and heartened by the stylistic range and breadth of topical interests that came to the fore: from Lynn Freed's brilliant, fable-like "Sunshine" with its inexorable and unforgettable conclusion, to Gina Frangello's wrenching coming-of-age story, set in vibrant 1980s Chicago, "Slut Lullabies," to Melissa Fraterrigo's subversion of the traditional predator-prey relationship in "Lil," to Amina Gautier's, Alison Umminger's, May-lee Chai's, and Cris Mazza's subtle but scathing examinations of the abuse of sexual power in academia in their stories "Preferences," "Something Transcendent at the Heart," "In an Academic Grove," and "Former Virgin," respectively, to Joan Frank's "A Good Plan," where on a train from Paris to Turin, notions of couplehood are examined and compellingly unbalanced, to Rebecca Entel's and Rachel Swearingen's beautifully wrought stories that frame moments where violence has touched or come harrowingly close to touching their main characters' lives.

In Victoria Patterson's "Superman," a young boy learns his mother's most devastating secret, and it's clear neither of them knows how to overcome its implications. In Karen Bender's "The Elevator" and Jenny Shank's "Comeback," we meet female characters whose bodies have been handled and exploited as if there weren't actual consciousnesses inhabiting them (it seems indisputable that an assailant's modus operandi is to ignore the victim's humanity), and I found myself thinking about how the unwanted touch or act of sexual aggression is a kind of robbery, but unlike a stolen handbag, you can't overcome the assailant's actions (or the lingering psychic toll) by replacing your money and purse. You have to carry the transgressive memory like a kind of dirty currency for as long as your brain and body hold onto it.

Christine Sneed
Pasadena, CA

The Elevator

Karen E. Bender

She was riding the elevator to her first job, as an assistant at a music magazine; the world fell away as she rose to the fifteenth floor. She was twenty years old. During the few months she had worked in this office, she had learned how to move names from column A to column B for event invites, make a collated set of Xerox copies, carry a cardboard box full of six different coffee orders. There was something remarkable and sparkling about all of it, the fact that, each morning, she entered the waiting room and did not have to remain there like the others, but was allowed to walk through the doors into the crammed gray hallways. The glaring fluorescent lighting stretched across the ceiling, the glass-windowed offices surrounding the main area like individual aquariums—she loved all of it. Entering the offices was like walking into a stranger's enormous, beating heart. She went to work each morning hoping the editors might soon trust her with more interesting tasks, for she wanted to show them everything she was capable of, which was endless and vast; however, each day they asked her, barely looking at her, to do the same dull things. But today she wanted to change the editor's view of what she could do. She was going to ask for more responsibility. She had practiced this, with her roommate, was thinking about how to set up an interview with the lead singer of the Go-Go's, if she should just call the musician's publicist or ask the editor first.

It was a slightly shabby elevator, in need of renovation, with the feel of a bathroom from the 1970s, the pink artificial marble-like panels faded, like almost invisible veins. The carpet was the color of a pale sky and always held the bitter odor of cleaning chemicals. The doors closed. She stood, examining the numbers flashing on the strip at the top of the elevator, and was only vaguely aware of a man standing in the elevator with her, and that they were alone.

The man turned to her and said, "I could rape you."

Her thoughts, curving in one direction, stopped. They looked at each other. He smiled, as though this were a joke. An iciness flashed through her. She was new to office buildings, and she didn't know—was this a joke men in offices made?

He was of indeterminate age, perhaps forty or fifty. The age in which men developed a soft, vulnerable chin. His skin was a pinkish shade of pale, as though he never got out in the sun. The low lights in the elevator made him look glazed, made of ceramic.

She remembered how he looked at her then, rapt, as though this was a discussion they had been having.

She remembered wanting to ignore this statement and get back to her previous thoughts, but her thinking had been stopped by this. The man moved toward her and she stepped back, and he touched her shoulder in a way that appeared strangely paternal, except for the fact that his other hand reached over and squeezed her breast, just for a moment, feeling it as though he wanted to test its presence. She felt her body gasp. She understood that, in this moment, anything could happen. The elevator doors opened. He darted out without looking back. The doors closed and she was alone in the elevator now, which slowly took her to the fifteenth floor.

So many years ago. It happened so quickly. Sometimes she wondered if she had imagined it. But why would she imagine someone saying anything like that? But since that time, whenever she found herself alone in an elevator with anyone, she got out. She got out even when she was with her children, when they were young, eight, ten, if it was just them and a man she did not know on the elevator. She noticed when people were getting off floors. A hot cloud rose in her, though she appeared calm; she would grab her children's hands and step onto the wrong floor while the person inside stood, watching.

"This isn't our floor," one of the children would point out.

She pretended not to hear and then said, "Oh. Wait a sec."

Slowly looking around, waiting for the elevator door to close. Sometimes the man inside would try to be polite and hold the door for her, waiting for her, waiting for her to step back inside, which was not what she wanted.

"Don't wait, go ahead," she'd say, waving her hand.

She would wait for the doors to close.

She had ridden many elevators in her life. When she graduated from college, she rode one to the twenty sixth floor of the publicity firm here she worked as an assistant. When she got married, she worked at a company on the sixteenth floor. When she had her first child, she was still at that company, with that terrible supervisor who promoted the coworker who sat on his lap when he asked her to; she remembered walking by the supervisor's office and seeing the woman perched on the edge of his leg, and occasionally she heard laughter that sounded like bullets were hitting the wall. Then she left that company and worked on the twenty-sixth floor of another building, a very fast, almost brutally efficient elevator, which never made any sound. It whisked her to the floor where many of the employees seemed to be sleeping even when they were perfectly awake. Somehow, this brought out a more authoritative part of herself, and she listened as she told people what to do, and often they followed her direction. Trying to wield this authoritative voice in other places—in the kitchen, in doctor's offices, in principal's offices—trying to press down the words slowly, to sound calm. The way the world came at you. The way hearts gave out, the way children had their own plans. The feeling of always wanting to know what to say, to be prepared. That office, on the twenty-sixth floor, was in New York City, a very tall, dark granite building with a view of Broadway facing north from Thirty-Fourth street, and the lights trailed out, bright necklaces, glittering strands that she wanted to grasp and climb like ropes. So she pulled herself along, year after year.

The company where she worked for the longest period, ten years, was on the thirty-seventh floor. She had become a senior editor at a textbook company, overseeing history books for middle grades. She was proud of the way she shaped the textbooks. She could tell the students what about the past was important to remember. Sometimes she thought back on the moment when the man on the elevator had turned and looked at her. She thought about that deliberate, unexpected shaping of that day. What had he gained, for himself, with that action? When she had walked off that elevator, she had, in some automated version of herself, walked to the assigning editor to ask her how to interview the music star. She did not remember what the editor had announced.

She felt the city, the pounding of steel cranes, construction, the watery swish of cars, vanish as she rose to her places of employment, as she stood in the rising elevator, a sensation, in the soles of her feet, of both lightness and fear. The numbers flashed in elevators all over the nation, in Los Angeles, in San Francisco, in Atlanta and Miami and Houston and New York, the elevators all somehow united in this cause, taking people up and up and up and up to some bruised version of their usefulness, or simply the slow shuffle through each day, all of these elevators rising as people stood, eyes gazing at the numbers above the doors, the oddly human sound of inhaled breath as the elevator rushed through the chute, as the employees were lifted to the floors where they worked, to the seats that they claimed, to the windows they gazed through, as the sunlight hit the city, the buildings glinting in the radiance like columns on fire.

The memory of that moment in the elevator dissipated, buried under the tumult of her life, but it was maintained in her bones, in the structure of her posture, for when she stood in elevators, there was always this subdued alertness.

One day, when she was in her mid-forties, past the time when she was perceived as a young woman but not quite sliding toward being old, she was in an elevator, heading to a meeting. She was thinking about the fact that she had to check out a statistic about casualties in the Battle of Gettysburg. So she did not notice when the elevator had let out people on the thirtieth floor.

And then on the thirty-first floor, the elevator lurched, as though it were a heart beating irregularly, and with a perverse, cheerful whistle, stopped.

She put her hand on the elevator wall to steady herself. There was a sound like water rushing outside of the elevator, but there was no water anywhere. She waited.

The door did not open.

"What the hell," he said.

There was one other person in the elevator.

He was bent over, his hand rummaging through a briefcase. He was tall, taller than she was, perhaps six feet. She saw the flash of his arm, but not his face. She had not been aware of anyone here. How had she been so absent, just then? She had a meeting to attend, how could she not have been aware? The elevator was about eight by eight feet. She had never really perceived it as a space before. The gleaming bronze panels, the ads framed in glass. Prix fixe at Restaurant Villa Grande on Floor Twenty-Seven. The free six-month membership at the health club on the Concourse. The plea to come and explore Costa Rica. She wanted to step into these ads, out of here, out of the space that was sealing her in.

She wanted to get out of the elevator. She pushed the door.

The thought crossed her mind that she could kill him. It was an impulse, an idea that rose from her gut before she could understand it. She was startled by the sudden and savage logic of this thought, how it could rise so quickly in relation to another person. How certain she was that he would try to attack her. The intensity of this thought embarrassed her, as though she understood the tenderness that gave fruition to it, the way she cherished her own life.

She banged on the elevator door with her left fist and then fumbled through her purse. All she had that approximated a weapon was a ballpoint pen. Her purse revealed some tawdry, ill-conceived faith in human nature. The elevator door made a deep, echoing thud as she hit it, and the doors remained shut.

"What the hell," she said.

She listened to her voice. Did it make her sound powerful? The concept itself seemed a joke.

She jabbed the Emergency button on the panel but it did nothing.

She did not want to look too closely at the person beside her. Perhaps if she kept staring at the lights on the elevator, he would stand, frozen, as well.

She banged on the door again.

The smell of orange gum and bacon. What was it? The odor of his breath. There was no place for breath to vanish here. He coughed.

She had not felt fear the first time—there had been no time to feel anything. Now it rushed up, a hot force, her heart turning over and over, her entire being wanting to get out of here, away, to pour through the solidity of these elevator walls. She wanted to hit the doors so hard they broke open. Her fear was embarrassing, and for this to be visible seemed shameful, would reveal her as crazy, and she was not. She was a deliberate, organized person. She had worked hard in her life and she was proud of the textbooks her company created, she was proud of what students learned from them; she had attended her children's dance performances and purchased school supplies and driven her family from one place to another. The heat charged through her throat, her arms, her face. She did not even know where it was rising from. She pretended to laugh—a hoarse sound, like a scrape—thinking perhaps that would defuse the situation, even though she knew nothing about the man standing in the elevator with her, could not describe the discussion they were having, silently, in tis elevator, without looking at each other. But they were having this discussion, of course, standing here, staring at the elevator doors, which remained, solidly, shut.

Open, she thought, looking at the doors. *Open.*

She thought she would walk out, whole, untouched; the doors would just open and she would walk out.

Sit down, she told him in her mind. Sit down. Like a child. Perhaps she could convince him. Go. Marry someone. Drive to Utah. Support public schools. Watch TV. Eat popcorn. Go outside and walk. Listen to me.

What was he saying to her in his mind? She didn't know. She listened to the wet sound of chewing.

There was a rustling and he moved and there was a sense of crystal breaking inside her chest as she darted back and he banged on the elevator door.

"Somebody!" he yelled. "Open up!"

From the back, he appeared young. Perhaps twenty. Twenty-five . He was wearing a navy suit; it did not fit him well; the jacket stretched across his waist and was a little baggy in the shoulders.

"Jesus," he said.

He turned toward her. His expression was not threatening; nor was it comforting. She wanted to place him, quickly, but she could not. He was in a rush. He looked like he had shaved, with purpose, this morning; his face was pinkish, raw. He banged on the door again and the elevator walls shuddered.

"Come on!" he called.

He was probably over six feet tall, soft, almost feminine around the waist and hips. He glanced at her, for a moment, as though he were waiting, in a hopeful way, for her to protest his banging, but she wasn't going to get into that.

She stood, half on the balls of her feet. They felt light; fear had emptied them.

"Push the Emergency button," he said to her.

She looked at him. She didn't like the way he spoke to her. Push. The button was on the panel beside her. She had already pressed it.

"I did," she said, icily. She pushed the button again, and there was a high, wheezing sound, as though some essential circuit had broken. "Look."

She saw him step toward the button panel; she quickly stepped back. He leaned forward and pushed it, too.

"No, he said. "Dammit. No."

She felt protected, somehow, by her age, the idea that she was too old, too wilted now, to attack; but perhaps she was just thinking this to comfort herself.

"They're fucking going to fire me," he said. He jabbed the Emergency button again.

He assumed she was listening. She pushed down the reflexive urge to comfort him, to say anything. He was not the man who had spoken to her those many years ago. But what had been left on her, the residue over all those years, was the idea that he could be.

This man in the elevator was anxious; she could see that, his glossy, dark hair a little damp around his forehead. His lips were red as though he had been eating a Popsicle, his features brisk, alert as though filled by a gust of wind in the back of his head.

He pushed the button one more time, and there was the long, hoarse shriek the button made.

"What a fucked-up building," he said. He staggered back and leaned against the wall. "Why are you so calm? Don't you want to get out of here?"

She couldn't help it; she almost laughed. She didn't answer.

"Don't you?"

She stared at him. She could say nothing. She put her palm against the elevator door in case she could feel a vibration, a prelude to the doors opening, when she could jump out.

He squinted at her, as though the elevator had gone dark. It was painfully bright, actually. There was a chandelier in this elevator, perhaps some perverse person had tried to imagine this metal chamber as a living room. She noticed, for the first time, that the chandelier was broken, two of the dangling crystals chipped. The light from the chandelier glared so she could almost see the shadow of the skull in his face; she wondered if he could see hers as well.

He sighed, sharply.

"They're going to kill me," he said. "Do you hear me? They. Are. Going. To. Gut. Me."

The last sentence made her jump a little; she gripped the ballpoint pen in her purse.

He slid down so he was sitting on the dusty floor of the elevator and rubbed his hands over his face.

She watched him. She was taller than he was at this moment. She wondered if she heard signs of life outside the elevator, or if she was imagining, the rumble of footsteps, a door slamming, a woman's laugh. But it felt as though the world had vanished, leaving only this cramped elevator stall, the golden walls gleaming in the relentless bright light from the golden chandelier. She had never quite noticed the golden walls of the elevator, how their grandeur implied some innate failure about the people riding it, how the riders would see, out of the corners of their eyes, blurred, gold reflections of themselves.

The man was speaking into the palms of his hands. "They said be there at three p.m. on the dot with photos or don't come in. Fuckers. I just know Smith planned this. I bet she's stopped the elevator right now."

She stood, silent.

He released a deep sigh. "Smith! I see you. You cunning bitch. You can't do this! I'm watching you right now."

He spoke the words directly to the elevator doors. His anger toward Smith seemed like a form of longing. She felt he was waiting for her to ask a question about Smith. It was a hunger she could feel, palpably, in the elevator, and, as a mother, was familiar to her. His own mother had, it seemed, ignored or belittled him.

She stood, sensing that hunger all around her, and with enormous effort, she did not answer it.

She was aware of her own hunger, huge, yawning inside her, to get out of here. She needed to get to her meeting. Today they would discuss ways to organize information about the end of the Civil War. The supplementary online material linked to chapters in the textbook, what was the budget and who they would hire to write it? The regular plans, how luxurious they now seemed. The staff was probably talking about her now, wondering where she was. She was ridiculously punctual, never absent or even late. But she was not afraid in the same way he was; well, she was, a little, but she was one of the senior people in the company, which protected her from the consequences of being late. The broken elevator was, after all, not her fault. They would, she assumed, be worried, but someone from maintenance would apologize, she thought. Are you all right? They would ask. I hate getting stuck in elevators. They would think it an inconvenience. They would not think of the others in the elevator with her, the travelers in this small, close space lifting eyes to their particular destination.

He was afraid, for other reasons, and she sensed his fear, thick in the air. She felt relieved and fortunate; her fellow employees would, she believed, not punish her for her absence. She was, she thought, not in the same situation that he was in, and understood that she could not reveal this to him.

"She planned this," said the man, a little hoarse. "You know? I could see it when she was sitting at her desk just staring into space and pretending to do nothing, but she was. I know it. Thinking about me."

She watched him gaze out at the elevator doors, staring at whoever was on the other side. What was this Smith doing right now? She imagined a woman in a trim black suit walking quickly down a hallway, holding her coffee away from her. Did this Smith, whoever she was, think of him, or notice him, or even know who he was? She remembered all the times she had thought of the first man in the elevator, and how she wanted to erase him from her mind, and wondered if perhaps that was part of what he had intended, to remain in her mind in that way, to establish this, a presence.

Her heart was still marching, full, and she was alert. He was still sitting on the floor, his long legs stretched in front of him.

The space held a peculiar, motionless heat, a dead, quiet airlessness. The elevator hung over a long, dark chute, nineteen floors above the ground. It did not move, but she was aware that they were standing in a fragile metal box, glancing at their golden selves as the elevator was suspended in the stale air.

He glanced up at her. "Why don't you say anything?" he asked.

She was not going to answer. She was going to stand there; his palm made an imprint on the gleaming elevator doors.

He regarded her, his eyebrows lifted. He was, she thought, trying to figure something out. Perhaps she thought she was deaf. Should she pretend to be deaf? Maybe she should pretend she had a disease. Didn't people do that, sometimes, to dissuade others from approaching them? On the elevator door, her hand was just barely trembling.

She could sense him, wanting her to speak, so that he would not be alone in this elevator. She understood, though she did not share this—he did not want to be alone. It had only been a few minutes, but it seemed the rest of the world had become nothing. Its presence was quiet and unknown. But she liked not speaking. He knew nothing about her. What was he guessing? Whom did she resemble? Did he think she was his mother, his sister, his girlfriend, what? Her own life felt like an exercise in deception.

There was the meeting she was about to lead, the glorious and unsettling moment when the staff, assembled around the table, clutching Styrofoam cups of coffee, eyeing the rubbery muffins on a paper plate, waited to hear what she had to say. The theater of the meeting itself, the fact that some people were assigned lesser positions, paid less money, even if they were smarter, or even better at their jobs, the heavy and living silence about this inequality, the fact that they all sat around the conference room, nibbling at the crackers and grapes, pretending that no one was aware of this. The fact that she sat at the head of the table now, and that she was the one to call a meeting to order, that she tried to turn the direction of the company the way she wanted, that the other employees asked her for direction, even if perhaps they resented what she had said. She was the first woman at her company to hold that position and she found the view from her place at the table was like gazing across a long, troubled sea.

The man sitting on the floor was looking at her.

"I've seen you," he said.

"What?" she said.

"I've seen you with her. In the hallway. Yep. Sixteenth floor."

He examined her with a new shrewdness, a desire to figure something out.

"I don't work on the sixteenth floor," she said.

"Yes, you do," he said, sitting up. "You know her. Tell her I'm coming. I'm going to be at work. Tell her not to worry. I'm late because I had to buy the car. It's not my fault. Sheila said buy the car. I didn't want the car, I didn't want more payments, for fuck's sake, student loans. She wanted to ride in it. So I bought it. I'm not going to be late. Tell her. Come on. You're best friends, right? Tell her."

He was sitting straight up against the elevator, his face wounded with misunderstanding.

"See, I know," he said, "She probably texted you a few minutes ago to ask, is he in there, is he in the elevator and you said, yes, in fact, he is—"

"I don't know what you're talking about," she said. "And you're wrong. I don't work here."

She listened to herself speak.

"I'm never here," she said. "I'm never in this building."

Her body became still as she said this, for this statement, though false, described something she understood. She sometimes believed that she was not in fact in this building or this elevator or even in this precise body or life. Her actual arms and chest and legs felt almost weightless as she said this, adjusting to this new reality.

"I've seen you," he said, trying to look her in the eye.

"It wasn't me," she said, her voice louder as she went on, "It was someone else. I'm security. They called me. I'm here—I'm here to make an arrest."

He blinked, uncertainty unfurling across his face. She was right about something. He had done something he felt guilty about, whether it was criminal or not. He looked away; everyone is pierced by a form of guilt.

She wondered where the original man on the elevator was now, after thirty years; perhaps he was in a nursing home. Perhaps he was dead. She imagined him buried, a lawn stretched, a green haze, over him.

"There was a disturbance. Seventeenth floor," she said.

He rubbed his palms slowly over his thighs, as though trying to warm his hands.

"I didn't hear anything," he said.

"Half an hour ago," she said. "You didn't hear it. You weren't here. Well, we got a call. There was screaming. The secretary called us. There was screaming."

This was exactly what had happened. A part of her felt certain of this, even though none of it was true. This new reality presented itself to her as a clear relief. Her face was hot, but she hoped he could not detect anything true about her in the crushingly bright light of the elevator.

"Don't you hear them?" she asked.

"What the hell are you talking about?"

She laughed, and that time, it sounded like a human laugh.

"I hear them," she said.

Standing by the elevator, she pressed her cheek to the golden doors. There were sounds, perhaps; running, the precise heaviness of masculine footsteps, the whine of a vacuum. Or nothing.

"Bullshit. Who do you hear? Who?"

She was not going to answer him.

"Sloan, it was Sloan I bet," he said. "Idiot was under so much stress. I saw him here yesterday, he looked like he was going to have a heart attack. Was it Sloan?" He tapped his fingers against the floor, almost joyful. They made a sound like mice running. He paused.

She held still, not saying.

"No it wasn't," he said. He stood up. "It was my girlfriend, she screamed this morning before she got out of bed, I made her scream, I'll tell you—"

He was standing beside her. His voice was heavy, as if a boulder were sitting on a piece of paper. His eyelid twitched.

"Not a scream like that," she said. "No."

He was silent.

"What? Was someone killing someone?"

Her cheek twitched; then she forced herself to look up, into his eyes. They were brown. She had expected them somehow to resemble a lizard's, but actually they looked more like a cat's, or actually, like neither. She said, quickly, "There was an attempt. There was a lot of blood. There will be many arrests."

Her voice came out louder and flatter than she expected. He lurched back. There were surprising dark shadows blooming under his armpits. He banged on the door another time, and the door thunked so loud she could feel it in her face.

"That's not fucking true," he said, looking at her. "That's not—"

"It's true," she said. "You don't know anything."

"What the hell do you mean?"

"I know everything," she said, softly.

"You do? So what are they going to do now? In fifteen minutes?"

She heard something else, the thinness of his voice, as though he had been shouting forever. It seemed thin as silk.

"They're on their way," she said, firmly. She had no idea, but felt certain she was right. It was, perhaps, what they both wanted to hear. "They're on their way. I hear them."

She pressed her body against the cold elevator doors. She listened, and there were no distinguishable sounds on the other side, nothing that told her about life out there, or whether anyone was coming to open the elevator, or working in their respective offices, or was present in the world at all; but there it was, she thought, the sound, a low roar, the almost perceptible gargantuan power of the machinery of this building, a faint whirr, if not of screaming, of relentless hunger, of something else. The man in the elevator also pushed his shoulder against the door. He was facing her. He was perhaps two feet away. His cheek was pressed, with all of its weight, against the golden door, and his eyes were closed as he tried to listen to the screaming she claimed was on the other side. The broken chandelier above them flickered; it looked like it was about to go out. She was cold. The elevator doors were cold.

She imagined, with envy, the day happening outside this building, the sun moving with its heat and brightness through the sky, and the shadows of clouds falling across the buildings, the sky blossoming from blue to yellow to orange to red to a darkness that revealed stars. She was not here, not in this place, not in any enclosure; she was here, with this strange package of herself, wanting to be out there, out there; she wanted to be everywhere in the world; she did not know how to get there. The smell of the man's orange gum was sickeningly sweet. She watched the man, his fingertips touching the door, waiting for a trembling, a vibration, waiting for sounds to indicate that someone was coming to open the doors and let them out.

In an Academic Grove

(after Ryunosuke Akutagawa)

May-lee Chai

The following transcripts are from interviews conducted by the University Counsel in charge of compliance for a Title IX inquiry.

The Chair

It's the strangest tale I've ever heard. I've known Buster for years and I've never had a problem with him. He's done so much for the program. He's funny. He's very warm. He's so accomplished. The students love him. His classes are always full. He works so hard. He's always thinking of what he can do for the program, for the students. He created the reading series. He invites such interesting speakers. He spends so much time with the students. They love how he thinks outside the box. Have you heard him read? He's such a great reader! He makes everyone want to write poetry. I've heard nothing but compliments. He has quite a few followers among the students. They adore him! They're practically groupies. They'll follow him anywhere. And he always champions the underdog. He's been such a good mentor. Taking students under his wing. He's a real asset to the program. Most of our students are first generation university students, as you know. They aren't used to having mentors. They really like it when a member of the faculty takes an interest. I remember that time he took them on a field trip to the desert to read their poems under the stars! And the time he drove a van to Yosemite. The students were talking about it for months afterwards. I mean, if [the poet] was the kind of person who'd do something inappropriate you'd think that's when he'd do it!

Why, no, I never heard a single complaint from any of the students.

No, why would I ask them that? That hardly seems appropriate.

Witness Number 11

Um, what time did I hear the shouting? Let me think. I was still in my office. It was the last day of winter quarter. The afternoon. I'd been working on finishing my grading before break. My husband and I were going to drive up the 1. I wanted to get all my work done before we left so I wouldn't have anything hanging over my head. I was ready for vacation. It was probably a little after three in the afternoon. I know I finally left at four-fifteen because I wanted to beat the traffic. I had hoped to wait until they were finished, I could hear [the poet]'s voice. His voice was quite loud. I had my door shut, but still. The shouting went on for quite some time. I didn't dare leave my office. I was hoping they would stop. It went on for at least an hour. Finally, I realized I needed to go or I'd be stuck on the highway for rush hour. So I just made a dash for it. They were both in the hallway, facing each other.

No, I couldn't make out anything specific. But their voices did sound contentious.

The Poet

Yes, I might have raised my voice. I didn't think I was being heard. No, I didn't mean "by the witnesses"! Do we have to use that word? Eleven? Good god! What kind of witch hunt is this?

Excuse me. What I meant, what I meant when I said I didn't think I was being heard, was I meant, I wasn't heard by Professor Lin. I meant, you know when you talk and someone just doesn't want to hear what you're saying, just doesn't want to listen to someone else's point of view. That's what I meant. This is the part that gets me. I have done so much for this program. I have done so much to put this program on the map. I have done so much for this department. And I do it because I believe in the students! They inspire me! Everything I do is for them! So forgive me if I got a little passionate, and my voice might have gotten a little louder. And someone who didn't know what was going on, someone who didn't care to listen, might have misunderstood what I was saying. What I was saying was my genuine concerns for the department. Claudia just did not want to hear. Claudia just did not want to hear what I had to say. But I did not shout at her! I was not shouting at Claudia! I was merely expressing my passion for the program that I have worked so hard for so many years to build! And I do not get the credit. The women in the department do not give me the credit that I deserve. They did not feel the way that I feel. They do not care about the program. They do not care about the students. Not the way that I care!

And so I may have gotten a little passionate! And when I'm passionate, my voice gets a little louder! But that is because I care so much!

No, I did not chase Claudia down the hallway. I followed her, it's true, because I wanted to talk to her. I wanted to explain to her so that she understood. Because she was not listening to me. She was not listening to what I was saying. But I did not "block" her. That is not true! She was free to go as soon as I was done explaining my feelings. I didn't block anyone! I was not threatening her!

I would never threaten Claudia! I'm not that kind of guy. I did not raise my fist. I would never do that. I might have raised my hands. I'm a passionate guy when I speak. I make gestures. But a fist? No way.

You see, you see how my voice naturally carries when I am feeling passionate? I'm a big guy. I'm a tall man. I admit it. Sometimes my voice carries like that. But that's why I always try to smile when I talk, when I explain my perspective. Because I know I'm a big guy.

I have no idea why Claudia would say what she said. I'm blindsided. I'm actually deeply hurt. I've always had nothing but respect for Claudia. I argued for her to be hired. You know, the chair didn't want to hire Claudia. The chair wanted the other candidate. The chair didn't think Claudia was as well published. The chair thought Claudia was a little long in the tooth. That's what the chair said, not me. The chair thought it was strange that Claudia hadn't gotten a tenure track job before now. But I argued in favor of Claudia. I thought it would be good to bring in a woman of color. Bring in some diversity. I thought our students would appreciate her. I thought it would be good to give a woman of color the opportunity to work with us, in our program. In fact, I convinced the chair to hire Claudia. This is what's so ridiculous about this situation. If anything, Claudia should be grateful to me. Very very grateful.

Professor Claudia Lin
[redacted]

The following account appeared as three blank pieces of paper in the file of the University Counsel. When held over a lighted candle in a completely dark room, however, words began to appear on the sheets, exposed by the alchemy of heat, smoke, and bitterness. The following is typed from the committee member's memory.

The Ghost of Claudia's Childhood Soul Who'd Liked to Read

When Claudia was a child, her parents' arguing was the soundtrack playing in the background of her mind. The low bass rumble of her father, her mother's soprano arias. She turned on the television to drown out the sound of their battling voices, the laugh tracks of the sitcoms punctuating their misery and recriminations. The narratives were of no particular importance. They were always the same. Her father's worklife, the complaints about colleagues and supervisors, the daily grind of humiliations, the mockery of his accent, the aspersions cast on his very self, his height, his appearance, the thwarted aspirations, the powerful drive of his will to overcome all, to work and work and work. Her mother's family woes, the sisters in need of money, calling their older sister, pleading for money, complaining about the husbands who beat them and their children, the husband who stole and sold the furniture, the car that broke down on the way to a job interview, the husband who needed bail. Because they shouted in Chinese, Claudia could not follow the details. They fought, Claudia assumed, mostly about money, but later she realized money had only been the catalyst.

Claudia's escape was the books she read. Once every two weeks Claudia's mother took her to the library and Claudia checked out the maximum number of books allowed from the children's section, carrying them home in a canvas bag, then reading and re-reading them every day, the characters' problems so much more vivid and real than her own. When her father burst upon her in the family room, TV playing in the background,

Claudia hunched over her book at the end of the couch, nearest to the light, her younger brother splayed on his belly on the floor, playing with his toy soldiers, it was reading that drew her father's fury. "What are you? Some kind of princess! Get up! Get up!" he shouted. There was something apparently that needed to be cleaned.

Claudia looked up, blinking, alarmed. She jumped to her feet, and started dusting the knickknacks on the shelves and then her father disappeared again into another part of the house, and her mother appeared, and Mom was furious about other things, things that had happened long ago when she was still a girl living in her own parents' home, long long ago, before Claudia was born.

Claudia's mind turned to the plots and twists of her book: Nancy Drew and George and Honey were trapped in a cellar. This was the fifth time in eight books they'd been trapped in a cellar or an attic. In three books they'd been taken to abandoned houses. In two they'd been lost in a wood. There was a pattern that was comforting, and a clear resolution, unlike her parents' fights which evolved and grew and elongated and surpassed any clear narrative form.

Claudia the reader. It was how she was seen in the family. Her Ye-ye proclaimed at family gatherings the attributes of all the grandchildren. Cousin Erica was talented and could sing and dance, Cousin Michael was fast and clever and could make everyone laugh, her younger brother David was tall and strong, and Claudia "liked to read."

In college, teaching about literature was all she'd ever dreamed of doing. Reading books for a living, writing about the structures of the narratives that had occupied her mind.

But at work she found the same forces that had made her father shout at home at his family created a new narrative pull. She found the attention that men paid to her appearance, the remarks about her body, her gender—they accumulated at first like a coating of dust, then heavier like a blanket of snow, and still growing like weights that pulled at her limbs, like a new source of gravity. She struggled to get through the day, holding her head upright, pulling her body through the halls of her building.

The men who felt they could remark about her face.

The men who felt they could speak over her voice.

The men who felt they could command her full attention to listen to whatever they had to say the moment they had to say it and expected, what? Acquiescence? Praise?

The men who felt they could touch her at will.

The part that had liked to read died a little day by day, pecked to pieces by the pettiness of the everyday. Until the moment when the man chased her down the hallway because she'd dare to turn her back and walk away while he still wanted to talk and talk and talk.

Claudia opened her mouth and screamed, and I flew out, free.

Dudes, in Theory

Elizabeth Crane

Hi Larry, I'm not actually interested in you, I only swiped right because I thought it would be helpful for you to know that you look much better in your third photo down, the one where you're smiling.

Hi Mitch, I'm not actually interested in you, I only swiped right because I thought it would be helpful for you to know that you look much friendlier in your third photo down, the one where you're smiling.

Hi Rodge, I'm not actually interested in you, I only swiped right because I thought it would be helpful for you to consider adding a photo where you're smiling.

Hi Jamie, I'm not actually interested in you, I only swiped right because I thought it would be helpful for you to know that a blurry photo does not help us get any idea of what you look like. Was that your intention?

Hi Charlie, I'm not actually interested in you, I only swiped right because I thought it would be helpful for you to know that putting up a photo of yourself wearing a mask is not much better than putting up a blurry one. (And look – good on you, mask-wearing dude, but don't put that pic up as the first or only one.)

Hi John, I'm not actually interested in you, but I thought it would be helpful for you to know that a blurry photo followed by a photo of you in a mask does not help us get any idea of what you look like and if the only message on your profile is, *I'm really cool,* well, who would know. Subjective anyway but in my experience if you declare yourself cool, the likelihood is high that it isn't true.

Hi Jon, I'm not actually interested in you, but I thought it would be helpful for you to know that the focus on booze in all of your profile photos should be of concern to anyone who cares about you.

Hi Steve, I'm not actually interested in you, but I thought it would be helpful for you to know that you are too tan and you should see a dermatologist.

Hi Les, I'm not actually interested in you, but I thought it would be helpful for you to know that your gym pic is not sexy and that's a bad tattoo that doesn't mean what you think it means.

Hi Nicholas, I'm not actually interested in you, but I thought it would be helpful for you to know that your bathroom towel selfie is not sexy and that's a bad tattoo that doesn't mean what you think it means. Google exists for a reason.

Hi Christophe, I'm not actually interested in you, but I thought it would be helpful for you to know that every other dude and their grandfathers have pictures of themselves on boats, and that maybe there's a universe of women out here who care as little as I do about boats and whether or not you own one or have ever been on or seen one? That maybe there is another option that better reflects who you are, and that maybe, maybe, there are not as many women out here who think a blurry shirtless photo on what is probably someone else's boat is all the effort required to get your uninspired ass a date with the fine likes of us or any other good woman out there. My bad if there actually is a universe of women out there who love men on boats, who are like, hm, if I could just picture this guy on a boat, I could be interested in him. Maybe I just need to build a boat-free dating app. But maybe even the boat-going women of the world would like it if some of you tried harder.

Hi Chad, I'm not actually interested in you, but I thought it would be helpful for you to know that adding a big fish that you may or may not have caught, to your shirtless boat pic, does not help your cause.

Hi Javier, I'm not actually interested in you, but I thought it would be helpful for you to know that in addition to being not as interested in boats as these profiles might have an alien believe, many women are also as uninterested in mountain bikes.

Hi Sean, I'm not actually interested in you, but I thought it would be helpful for you to know that you should just keep your fucking shirt on.

Hi Eddie, I'm not actually interested in you, but I thought it would be helpful for you to know that when you tell a woman to 'be' anything, in your case and **in more than a few others 'fit,'** the only appropriate response is *Don't tell me what the fuck to be.*

Hi Ezra, I'm not actually interested in you, but I thought it would be helpful for you to know that I was intrigued by your profile when I saw the pic of you cuddling with a puppy only to learn that you think I should be 'youthful' and 'fit' so I think I'll go ahead and say no, Grandpa, I think *you* should be fit. But not for me, as I said, because I wouldn't fuck you either way.

Hi Tim, I'm not actually interested in you, but I thought it would be helpful for you to know that I was intrigued by the first few profiles of men cuddling puppies but then I saw this trick a hundred more times and then I came to yours that said you were apolitical and I feel like you really need to know that's not a thing. You may as well just go ahead and declare yourself an asshole. On the other hand, I guess it's good to know you won't ever try to argue with me about what I do with my body, like say have an abortion if I get pregnant by you, since you won't have any opinion about that.

Hi Andre, I'm not actually interested in you, but I thought it would be helpful for you to know that when you tell a woman to 'not be' something, in your case, Russian, the only appropriate response is не говори мне, что, черт возьми, не быть. I used Google translate for that so if it's wrong, on behalf of Russian women everywhere, fuck off.

Hi Josh, I'm not actually interested in you, but I thought it would be helpful for you to know that the photo of just your eyes, nose and forehead is absurd.

Hi Brad, I'm not actually interested in you, but I thought it would be helpful for you to know that the photo of just your mouth and chin is stupid, but there's a dude here with just a photo of his eyes, nose and forehead, and it seems like you guys might be a better fit for each other than you would be for any women out here.

Hi Lance, I'm not actually interested in you, but I am super curious about what you really mean in saying 'God-fearing seeks same' because to me that seems like no way to live? Does it mean you believe in an embodied, punishing god who's just waiting around for us to mess up, which then somehow motivates us to behave well? Is this about being punished in the afterlife? Or is it really that you think the godless or god-not-fearing among us can't motivate ourselves to behave well without fear? I truly don't get it, but maybe you're just weeding people like me out and the god-fearer you seek will find you and you can, I dunno, live a perfect, fearful life together.

Hi Antonio, I'm not actually interested in you, but your five-dollar-words are not going to get you a smarter woman, a smarter woman is going to run far away from a pretentious prick who calls himself a sapiophile and knows that one quote by Emily

Dickinson. We know your kind the best. Us smart women may not hang around with the shirtless seafaring crowd but we have been taken in by your kind a time or two and we're not twenty-one anymore. Quit it.

Hi Wayne, I'm not actually interested in you, but you're casting a very tiny net with those one square/one circle glasses frames.

Hi Kenny, I'm not actually interested in you, but when you specify 'no drama,' one has to wonder how there's any drama that you haven't also participated in. Otherwise you'd do better to specify 'no angry monologues,' but I doubt that would go well for you either. I doubt there's one woman out here thinking, Gosh that guy seemed perfect for me but I can't believe he doesn't like drama, oh well.

Hi Louie, so sorry to know that you and every third guy on here has had so much drama inflicted on them by the women in their lives. I'm so curious to know if there's an agreed-upon definition of drama among you, or if it's just a thing where a couple of your dates had an opinion you didn't share, or said no about one thing or another, and you had somehow reached your dating years never having had such an experience and were just so shocked when it happened that you ran away like a screaming toddler?

Hi Joe. Look, at this point, I'm bleary. Forgive me. The pix of you with your kids are genuinely sweet, you seem like you might even have a sense of humor, your paintings are actually interesting, very psychedelic Cy Twombly, and you get major kudos for not being shirtless on a boat. Your second photo is much more appealing than the broody one in front of the sculpture, which makes you look mean. But I find it increasingly hard to look past these frowning photos. What is your aversion to smiling? I started looking at women's profiles to see if we frown as much as this or do any number of other asinine things too, but no, our profiles are on balance so much more appealing than yours. I texted this to a friend and she texted back *do we like girls now* and I said *I wish because they are better but so far I still like dudes, in theory.* I have been trying to give this app thing more of a chance than I've been inclined to in the past. I was single for a long time, so single I wrote a book about being single, and then I was married for a long time and then I was divorced and then the country shut down just as I was beginning to think about dating again and we're slowly sort of kind of maybe emerging, and I haven't been touched by anyone besides my dog for over a year and I was hoping this would give me the wee bit of hope or willingness to put the effort in here. I took the time to curate my photos and considered how best to convey some small sense of who I am in this very limited medium. (I mean, I am extremely appealing, but I am no longer an extremely appealing young woman, I know this, I am an extremely appealing older woman, and many of the men that pop up interested in a woman who is appealing in this particular way (and there are some, yourself included, I have to give you that) are, well, not so appealing. I mean, is it fair of you to wonder if I have an inflated sense of myself, if my own profile is less enticing than I imagine it to be, or if my profile is extremely enticing but I myself am not so? Wonder away. I wonder about a lot of things, but not that. You would be lucky to have me.) And after swiping through all the fellows available to me, after 'expanding my search' (as you probably understand, this can mean looking farther than your immediate location, area or, more accurately 'lowering your standards') to allow in some conspiracy theorists and what have you, I've grown tired, Joe. Can't you just smile? Ironic that a feminist is asking this of a dude since it's pretty widely known women do not enjoy being told to smile by random men, and it stands to reason that men might not like being told by random women to smile, but that said, for fuck's sake at least smile for one fucking photo. I know a lot of dudes have a photo face, my husband had one, and I know he didn't think it was a scowl, but it kind of was. I also have a photo face. I smile. It's not a fake smile. It's just a nice, pleasant smile. Certainly, I have been photographed laughing, and I like some of those photos of me best. And when you are photographed laughing, chances are I like those photos of you best too. Whoever you are. Including you, Joe. I've said this many times but it bears repeating: I knew my husband for a year before I realized he was cute, and this is because it was a year before I saw him smile for the first time. You could be some really great guy, but I'd swipe away your broody photo face, and I would never know. But really, I can't tell from a photo or two if I would ever like any of you. Surely there's one or two among you that I might really connect with, were we to randomly meet in some non-app way, but at this point, you're all merging into one big blob of indistinct unsmiling heads and the reality is I never know if I'm interested in someone until after I've talked to them in person. And it seems like the only possibility here is to meet all of the blobby heads to find the one blob I'm compatible with. I am told that it's a numbers game, that you have to go on a lot of dates to find one good one, to which I say do what you want, but I just don't have the time. Someone once told me they sometimes went on three dates a day. Once, once, when I was younger, I had two dates in one day, and at least I knew I liked one of them. Three dates in a day? I can imagine no other outcome of this for me than the depths of despair. I don't want to go on one date a day. I have TV shows to binge. That's not actually a joke. Sitting across the table from a dude with a blurry photo who wants me to be 'fit' is not worth an hour of my life just on the extremely off chance that he's better than his profile indicates, or in focus he looks like George Clooney, and even

George wouldn't get a pass on that unless maybe I was out of my mind horny that day, and frankly, that seems unlikely. I honestly can't remember the last time I thought, I really want to have sex right now. Maybe I thought that once or twice when I was drunk, and I just don't remember. Otherwise I'm not sure I've ever had that thought. My thoughts have ranged from I definitely want to make out with that guy to making out with that guy to feeling like I might want to have sex with the guy I'm making out with, to I definitely do not want to have sex with the guy I'm making out with, or, I might want to have sex with the guy I'm making out with at a later time, or, I might want to have sex with the guy I'm making out with at a later time tonight, after we make out and maybe do other stuff until I feel sure that I do or don't want to have sex with this guy at any point tonight, to all I really want is to just spoon with this guy until I fall asleep and everything is okay, or at least until tomorrow. But these apps don't give me anywhere to say any of this, Joe. So I'm saying it to you. Is any of this agreeable to you? I'm guessing no. I'm not asexual. I looked it up. Legit asexuality is not considered a problem. It's just what you are. The only reading I can find on my current level of desire describes it in no uncertain terms as a problem. Which to me is the real problem. Every type of desire a person can have seems acceptable unless the desire exists and is minimal. And it seems like the primary reason we might want to 'solve' this 'problem,' Joe, is because we want love, and we all know that's hard enough, and we all know it's hard even when two people might have similar levels of desire but, you know, maybe I want to do it in the morning and you want to do it at night, or I have a particular kink for sex on Tuesdays at noon but something awful once happened to you on a Tuesday at noon, conflicts and other obstacles are always going to exist between two people, of course, but I guess what I'm wondering is what the chances are of any of us meeting someone with either our exact desire level or has a willingness to deal with the other person's exact desire level because how the fuck do you even compromise on that? What even is compromise when it comes to sex? Is that actually even possible? Am I overthinking this? I know I can live without sex, I'm pretty sure no living human would literally die without sex and I know I am free to say to any partner that I'm not in the mood. So if I'm never in the mood, but I'm willing to try to get in the mood, but only to a point, would that be cool with you, Joe? There's no box to check on this app for this 'interest.' There's a stupid fucking 'apolitical' box, but there's no box that says 'I'm tired, Joe, and I'm lonely and even if I do decide I want to do it with you, it might not be often, but the package deal includes a shit ton of laughs, thoughtful conversation, and when you are sad I will hold your hand.'

Look, I just got home from a mammogram, take that for what it's worth, something you want to do, but it's a torture device invented by a man, and the governor of the state of New York, my state, has been accused of numerous counts of sexual harassment by numerous women. Hard for me not to imagine if what his own asinine dating profile might look like (no doubt featuring one of the many photos out there of him on a boat with a fish): *60s but looks 40, divorced, father to daughters, four I think, rogueishly handsome, saved NY from the pandemic, interested in women my daughters age or younger.* Of course he didn't need one, when there were so many women right in the office there for him to wield power over, though now that he's out of office maybe I can look forward to being swiped left by him for being close to his own age. And here's me on this app, trying to reason with a dude defending his boat-bro governor by saying *I'm Italian, we're just like that* and *If a woman doesn't want it she can just say so*, and I'm good and even reasonable at arguing garbage arguments to a point, but it shouldn't be on us to say we don't like that shit, it should be obvious that you shouldn't fucking touch us without asking, asshole. So that guy and the governor can fuck right off into space. It's exhausting, Joe. I was a good partner to my husband. I thought I was. I did the best I could. I was kind and loving and supportive. And we had sex! So much sex! So much more than enough sex for me, and enough to tide me over until who knows when. I'm plenty tided over, Joe. I thought my marriage was going to be forever and it wasn't. It happens. And occasionally I have moments of compassion for all of us who are just lonely and want to meet someone, and moments of hope that someone else who's more appealing than their photo is as well tided over as I am and finds me. Passing moments. Then I go back to just wanting dudes to fucking do better. It's not your fault, Joe. I mean it kind of is, but not really. But yeah kind of.

The Swamp in Her Voice

Rebecca Entel

Margaret Thatcher isn't anyone's, but we want to be the ones to find her.

Dax wants to be the one more than I do. I look out at the grey bones of the trees and the drooping three o'clock sun – as if even I, five-foot-one, could grab it – and feel an empty belly of hopelessness.

"That dog's been missing for weeks, and there's supposed to be a snowstorm on Tuesday," I say. It was just Thanksgiving a second ago, but the earth can't seem to hold onto its warmth any more.

"We can't give up!" Dax says, retreating from his vigil at the edge of the woods. He pulls me back to the car by the sleeve of my puffer coat. This is the second weekend we've followed the map he created from the social media thread of sightings. Farther and farther into the countryside.

He drives; I watch. The stubbly spaces that will eventually again be corn fields alternate with woods and strings of beige new-builds with gleaming driveways.

"We don't even know her actual name," I say. Just that someone at the shelter where she was dropped has a weird way of acknowledging history or maybe loves deregulation.

"Keep watching," Dax says, clutching the steering wheel as if he could squeeze Margaret Thatcher out from behind the trees.

"I am."

Margaret Thatcher went from the local shelter to a foster home to get used to people, but her first weekend she escaped during a walk. It felt like the whole city was following the sightings on social media, threads pouring down with hope and grief and anxiety each time she ran away from another would-be rescuer. Even when it was two in the morning, Dax live-texted his scrolling through the photos, his phone auto-un-correcting all the things he thought could happen to a missing dog. Before my brain fully sorted out the jumble of nonsense words into his fears, I slid my phone under the mattress and crushed my face into the pillow.

But I look at those pictures as much as Dax does, especially when I can't sleep. Margaret Thatcher is toffee-colored, tall, and spindly, which makes her look deer-like, both wild and fragile. Her black eyes look like the wettest, ripest blueberries. No whites. The eight-year-old twins in my building chalked *please come home sweet sweet margaret thatcher!!!!!!* all over the sidewalk, and each day I've carefully stepped around every letter.

There have been three sightings in a forty-eight-hour period in this area west of town, so whoever's running the social media campaign begs every day for strangers to do exactly what we're doing.

He drives; I watch.

Dax starts narrating his daydreams about how it would feel to find Margaret Thatcher and bring her back to her foster home.

"Just think what everyone would say about us. Total strangers!"

I don't say this to him, but maybe he's obsessed with finding Margaret Thatcher because one middle-of-the-night years ago his half-brother found the kitchen glazed with fire and got, one, everyone out of the house; two, his name on the local news more than once; and three, a story the whole family told with drippy eyes for years. Or maybe it's because Dax was the one to let his roommate's cat out accidentally and RIP Bonkers. *Guilt can make you stretch to great lengths* is something my mom has said every time my father sends me money in an envelope with a different state's postmark.

The sky flashes and cracks, flashes and cracks, floods with darkness. The view through the windshield goes from speckled with dots to washed away. As the wipers squeak faster and faster, Dax pulls the car over into a Burger King parking lot.

"Shit," he says, posture collapsing, and we both sigh. I picture the neighbor kids' sidewalk chalk disappearing.

He stares straight ahead at nothing while I scroll through my old texts. Dax's worries mis-corrected by his phone – *word teams. poses searing your garage. haunted by a truce. swampy if being who. caught by a wring student* – harden into sense. The woods teeming with toothy animals and hunters, poisons seeping out of garbage, trucks on the highway going so fast they can't stop, the swampy part of the lake brewing who-knows-what, the hands of the wrong stranger. The story he's trying to avoid looks like bubbles floating up and up that never disappear.

When the rain finally thins from *whoosh* to a staccato, Dax gets out to swipe at the windshield with a towel he's kept in the backseat since his defroster stopped working, and I go inside to get a sack of food for both of us.

My bare hands numb against the cup I'm holding, the napkin wrapped around it thinned to nothing by the moisture.

"I just remembered something," I say, as Dax climbs in and reaches for the pocket of onion rings that's filled the car with its fried smell.

"About Margaret Thatcher?" Dax's chapped lips spread in anticipation, but when I shake my head, his voice becomes deflated. "Oh. Is this a story about Burger King?" Dax grew up in a family that never went out to eat and in a house without a TV, so even my dumbest childhood stories sound to him like one-ups.

I shake my head, mouth full, though it is the smell of this food – and especially that blank suction just before the straw released the first rush of strawberry shake – that brought the memory into the dome of the car.

We spent enough time at the Burger King by our house that my mom became friends with a woman who worked there. We'd see her in her uniform, rounding the booths with a spray bottle and towel as my mom and I sat on the low stools of the kids' table, watched over by flat animal sculptures that were only painted on one side. I could see where the woman's rag moved smoothly over a clean table and where it snagged on old soda spills. If she slowly gathered the rag by the table's edge, I knew she'd cup her other hand below to catch a gang of crumbs. The most noticeable thing about her was how her mouth was a tiny keyhole while my mom's spread across her face like a slice, mouth unhinging like a muppet's when she laughed. I never saw the other woman laugh, but we saw her in regular clothes each time she came to our house as the Avon Lady, with bottles and tubes in colors similar to the Burger King sign.

"Is this a story about your fancy mom who wears tons of make-up?" Dax asks, the tail of a fry disappearing into his mouth. We both laugh.

When I think of my mom, I picture her back as she walked toward the city bus that would take her downtown to work: her oversized windbreaker flapping around her, the way she leaned forward as she walked, her beige slacks and thick-soled brown shoes and ponytail of dark brown hair that sprouted, unruly and cottony, from its gathering in a red elastic band. The same each day. She paid attention to her appearance only when it came to a skin condition on her hands. I remember her standing in front of the bathroom mirror, balancing her Avon tubes on the sink with the metal legs. She applied lotions in endless loops while I watched from the hallway, since the bathroom couldn't fit us both at once. No one but me knew about her hands – me and the Avon lady, I guess.

That day in the kitchen, I left the two of them to discuss the samples and went outside where the Avon Lady's son was stalking our yard and the neighbor's, picking up sticks. His deep-set, angry eyes scared me, but I was one year older, which made me brave.

"You shouldn't go in our neighbor's yard. That's their property. Those sticks belong to them." A weird sense of ownership for a girl like me who lived on a block of rentals and who liked to tunnel through the overgrown patch behind the garage to cut across someone else's yard while the woman who lived there screamed and waved her cigarette at me.

"Can't you see," the son said, eyes and lips active, "that I'm trying to *do* something?"

"Is this a story," Dax asks, "about angry, scary boys?" He floats his fingers in front of my face like invoking something spooky, then plunges it down by my leg – reaching, I realize, for the paper bag crackling at my feet. I tell him it's just trash now, but he fishes out a stray fry and smiles smugly.

•••

We're on the highway again in just moderate rain, the car still full of the Burger King smell. My eye snags on any bit of movement that's not another car – promises that turn out to be a flattened cardboard box somersaulting in the wind, something that looks canine-ish until it lifts and glides toward the horizon.

After I lectured him, the boy had barked at me. Barked. Like a dog. Dax and I laugh. But at the time, I ran into the backyard.

I could see through the kitchen window that the Avon conversation was still going on. I got on the swing-set glider to feel the air stream through my hair.

"Did you just tell me that story because of the barking, just because of the dog? Or is this a story about you always choosing to be by yourself?" Dax turns toward me, suspicious and annoyed, as if I'd asked him to take me home to be alone, despite the storm and Margaret Thatcher, and to hell with his hero dreams.

I look at him, pausing, and wipe residual grease onto the napkin I'm holding that's still warmish from being in the bottom of the bag.

"It's not," I say, though I am ready to go home.

Dax's eyebrows tug upwards and his voice quickens. "Wait, does that boy wander off somewhere but then this is a story of someone finding him safe? Like we're going to with Margaret Thatcher?"

"What?"

His face settles back toward his chin. He keeps driving. I keep watching.

When I'd first moved here, those grown-up cornfields tricked my eye with corridors that seemed orderly, but their lines shot off at constantly-shifting angles as you drove by. The way in and the way out multiplied, which meant they disappeared. A terrifying place to get lost. Winter is on its way, though, so now the fields look rampaged instead of dense. I look toward the other side of the road.

"Wait, wait!" I shriek and point at a flash of movement slipping into the edge of trees. "There! Over there!"

The car shrieks off the cement at an almost ninety-degree angle, rumbling over the uneven ground and hard-stopping so that my body flings forward like a ragdoll and then back into the seat. Dax is running – door open, car dinging and dinging, me still buckled. He disappears into the trees but then reappears, scooping his arm through the air for me to join him. I can't hear what he's yelling.

When I reach him, I throw the keys at him. He's out of breath and pointing.

"All I saw by the time I got over here was a deer down over there, and then as soon as it saw me it ran away. Margaret Thatcher must've gotten spooked by it and taken off. So we should keep going to find her. She can't be that far! If we just go deeper in. She was *right here!* You saw her!" He points into the dark density of the trees.

Everything smells like mud that's been rinsed clean, but I can still smell in my hair the scent of crispy things gone soggy. Dax turns his back to me as he follows his own pointing arm, but then he swivels his neck and sees me standing still.

It's my mistake. I should've seen the differences in the tails. I should've looked more closely before I screamed anything.

"Come *on!*" He sounds angry.

I tell him it must've been the deer I saw. If a dog had been running in there, how would the deer still be standing there, if it was scared away by even a person approaching from afar? I saw a deer, not Margaret Thatcher.

"You don't know that for sure," Dax says in the same desperate voice, walking farther in but watching me.

"Even if we had any idea that she was definitely in there, I'm not sure we should –. I mean, how would we find our way back out of here?"

I look around at what must be the most landmark-free stretch of land I've ever seen. Nothing to mark where we are. No odd tree, no sign, no creepy house in the distance. Nothing. And we left the leash Dax bought in the car anyway.

"Dax."

"It's gonna get dark soon, Dax."

He's far enough in that I only see parts of him weaving in and out of trunks.

"Dax!"

I take a step toward him, trying to throw myself face-first into his story of spotting Margaret Thatcher, clipping a leash on her because she wouldn't run from *us,* showing up at the foster home with their precious cargo in the backseat of his car. I take another step into the trees and into his dream of the shining, adoring eyes that see we've brought Margaret Thatcher home with her ears relaxed and a hint of white rimming her eyeballs. Instead, in the reel in my head, I see her running away, showing us only her tail that's nothing like a deer's. I see darkness like a locked fist and teeming woods.

"Word teams," I say, quoting his text, to no response. He gives me the finger without turning around.

I watch until I can't see him and slog through the muddy grass back to the car.

Sitting on the hood, I'm ready to yell at Dax for how cold I am on top of everything. I sit there forever, watching for him to emerge from the trees, watching the time on my phone change and the service come in and out.

"You stuck, hon?"

A blue pickup is idling on the shoulder. The driver's wearing a baseball hat and has spiky grey hair wrapped around his face. He stays inside his truck but it's so close I can see his eyes are bulging and rheumy.

I don't say anything.

"I can pull you out of that mud if you're stuck." His arm points toward me and the car the way Dax had pointed toward his imagined Margaret Thatcher sighting, but the man's arm looks so much bulkier. His hand slab-like.

"Or give you a jump if that's it."

I look back for Dax, and it seems like the sun is slipping lower and lower. The sky's not even pink, everything's just grey. I clutch my phone in my fist, afraid to check whether or not it's getting a signal. The truck's grumble stays the same while a few other cars doppler by.

"Hey, you need help or what?"

I shake my head over and over and over until the truck finally pulls away.

I get off the trunk and sit behind the car where no one from the road can see me and where Dax will see me glaring at him when he comes back. If there's any light left at all when he does.

I keep the flashlight app on my phone off, but I keep reminding myself it's there. The wet from the ground seeps into the butt of my jeans.

•••

When Dax finally comes tramping toward the car, my jeans are soaked through, and it's too dark for him to look like anything but a shadow. Inside the car I can see he's angry and depressed-looking, his jeans splattered with mud and his shoes caked. He turns on the car without saying anything or looking at me.

When the sun had disappeared from our backyard that evening, quickly chilling the air, I'd gotten off the swing-set. I came in the side door, not letting the storm door slam so the boy wouldn't hear that I'd gone inside. From the doorway, where I tipped my shoes off with my toes, I could see my mother's back in her chair at the table, the same one she always sat in, and the Avon Lady standing in front of her, though her face was blocked by the archway of the breakfast nook. They didn't turn or indicate they'd heard me come in.

The Avon Lady was talking about what a man had said to her at work that day.

"'What's in this pocket?'" Putting one hand on her right hip. "'What's in this pocket?'" On her left. "'And what's in this pocket?'" Laying a hand over the fly of her pants.

I'd felt a blank suck of air as I stood still, trying not to make a sound. My ears felt plugged, and I couldn't hear what they said to each other next. I took a long time in the hall, lining my shoes up on the mat against the wall where my mom wanted them.

The Avon Lady's tired voice again leeched into the hallway, fretful about what to say to her son on a day like today, how much she should tell him about what had happened at work when he wouldn't let up, as he usually wouldn't, when she needed him to let up.

My mother's voice was low and layered. Sedimented, like something dredged up. "Can't you just tell him you had a bad day at work." She said it without a rise at the end of the question.

The door smacked behind me, the boy's body swifting by me into the kitchen to ask his mother when they were leaving. I followed behind him, my mother's back not twisting, and I saw the beats of our breakfast nook – the window with the pea-green curtain, the chair we never sat in stacked with mail, the fake wood grain of the table, my dead grandpa's broken camera that for some reason was our permanent centerpiece, and now two orange tubes and a boy with an armful of sticks – but not her eyes.

Dax is driving again, but the car is pointed back where we came from. The beams from the headlights find their edges.

"Is this a grab-them-by-the story?" His voice, his attention, a pulling-away kite whose string has slipped my grip, as if this is a story we've all heard before – which it kind of is, though back then, for me, it wasn't. *haunted by a truce.*

It's too dark to see anything, but I'm still watching out the window so hard there's a pull in my neck. Maybe it's not *home,* though, I want to tell Dax about his returning-her hero fantasies.

No one on social media or the news or in chalk or in this car is saying that to Margaret Thatcher, all the rescuers look like pursuers. I feel a blankness settling: the soaked land spreading out around us of all the places Margaret Thatcher isn't.

"No." This is a story about all the shadowed things my mother knew how to hide from me.

Slut Lullabies

Gina Frangello

I found out my mother was a slut from my best friend, at a bar with my secret Greek boyfriend who was possibly a homosexual and his uptight brother who pretended to know nothing of our affair. I was high on myself that evening. It was a buzz I got rarely—the way somebody who hardly ever drinks gets plowed after one sip. At eighteen, I had progressed from being a girl who never attracted much attention, to a woman who never attracted much attention—so this kind of evening, featuring me as the heroine of an illicit liaison, flanked by single, sexless friends who suspected but could not confirm my "other life," made me feel like a tingly imposter with all eyes upon me.

I was dancing, I remember that. My best friend Sera and my lover Gus were dancing with me—not with each other, or alone, but each trying to be my partner. Sera was fiercely jealous of Gus, not because she was either attracted to him or because she didn't like him, but simply because he claimed my attention, and she was not accustomed to having to compete. She was used to being the flower around which all the bees buzzed; used to feeling magnanimous for allowing me to be the Queen Bee fed of her charm, wit and loyalties on a priority basis, while others had to work hard. Gus's older brother George was hot for Sera, but this was of little consequence since he was a prematurely balding, stoop-spined twenty-two-year-old, who worked at their father's dry cleaners fifty hours per week, lived above the store, and had skin the color of flour-coated dough. If you yelled to him, "Hey dude, where'd you put the beer?" he would reply in a Spock-like voice, "I believe it is in the vehicle." He was weird, and while marginally sexy in a dark, mortician kind of way, definitely not Sera's type.

Sera and I were fond of bars. Though I was not prone to get drunk on my own sexual power (even the phrase seems absurd), I was quite known for getting inebriated on just about anything else. We'd had fake ID's since age sixteen, but we'd started drinking when we were twelve, stealing from my mother's bottles and picking up an extra pack of Benson & Hedges when she sent us to the store to buy hers. We were not "fast girls"—Sera was a virgin, and Gus was my first lover—but like many young women who came of age in the mid-eighties, we were heavily into partying, dancing, dressing to the nines even to sit around at McDonald's or study hall, and doing "everything but" with guys we picked up at parties, since dating per se (the way Sera's mother described it at least) did not much exist among our crowd. You made out once, and then you either automatically became boyfriend-girlfriend (which did not necessarily involve dates), or you carefully ignored each other for the remainder of your teenaged life.

"I'll stop the world and melt with you," Sera sang, shimmying her shoulders on the dance floor. Gus had told me once that he could tell she'd be good in bed because of the way she moved her shoulders when she danced. She was uninhibited, he said; he could tell. Since I was the first girl he'd ever slept with, I was unsure what made him such the connoisseur, but felt both oddly proud of Sera and flattered that he might be trying to make me jealous. "There's nothing you and I won't do!" She pointed at me and threw her arm around me—this song was laden with significance for us as it had played constantly in the discos during our senior trip to the Bahamas a few months prior. But my time in the Bahamas had been spent stealing away from my friends to sneak to Gus's room—he had even sprung for a single so we could be alone—and that Sera didn't know it made me feel treasonous to both of them, no longer giddy with my wriggling, sex-kitten abandon. So I stiffened, drew my arm away.

I don't remember the name of the bar. There were so many in those days. I don't remember what Sera and I were talking about, or how talking was even possible in the midst of her singing and competing with Gus for my dancing attentions (funny since I was not a very good dancer. Inhibited, I guess you could say), but somehow we got from point A to point B. Point A being that Sera suspected I was "totally in love with" Gus—something in her tone made me bristle as if wrongly accused—and point B being that she did not want to see me make the same mistakes my mother had. "I don't want to see you turn into your mother," was what she said, by which I thought she meant *divorced*. I figured she did not want me to marry Gus because she feared he would divorce me due to his family's disapproval. Though I'd never discussed this worry with Sera, I assumed that, as usual, she had read my mind. "Oh, we're just fooling around," I laughed, trying to sound worldly and laissez-faire to put her off. But Sera's pointed face puckered like I was something she had bitten into that had gone bad. "Emily," she said, somber amidst the music, "that's exactly what I mean."

My mother was popular. She had me when she was twenty, so when I was ten years old and she was thirty, she still had girlfriends—all single or divorced—who came over and smoked Benson & Hedges at our kitchen table, wearing silk blouses that revealed tan décolletage. They had bouncy, feathered hair like Charlie's Angels, long fingernails, numerous shiny gold chains, and sometimes three rings on one finger. My mother got us a discount on our rent from Tony Guidubaldi, our middle-aged, married landlord, who also had a plumbing business and more money than most of the men in the neighborhood, even the mobsters. She knew all the bartenders; she never had to pay for drinks, her friends teased. I was proud of my mother. My father had been a heroin addict and car thief. I had a dim memory of watching him shoot up, but my mother said he never did that in front of me and that I must be imagining it based on something I saw in a movie. Mom kicked him out when I was three, and she heard he went to jail shortly afterwards. Neither of us ever saw him again. My mother was like the women on the popular 70s sitcoms: *Rhoda, Alice, One Day at a Time*. Divorced, independent, spunky. She made Sera's parents, who were only a decade older than Mom, seem about a hundred years old.

Mom was initially upset about Sera, who, when we first met at ten, was bookish and fat. While we spent most of our time in my bedroom playing elaborate imaginary games that involved things like Charlie's Angels living behind my wall and Marie Osmond secretly being my mother, Mom surveyed with anxiety out the picture window of our ground floor apartment all the cool girls of the neighborhood, smoking their Newports and wearing their Italian jackets with red stars around their last names, blazened on the back. These girls, some only a couple years older than I, looked like mini versions of my mother's friends, and Mom ached for me to be one of them so I could have a good life. She encouraged me to dump Sera, saying I would look fat and nerdy by association (though I was a stick and didn't read much), but it was no use. I loved Sera with an intensity to which both my mother and I were unaccustomed—with the intensity Sera would later inspire in all our high school friends once she was no longer fat or buck-toothed or frizzy-haired, although still bookish, which had somehow become acceptable and even made her look a little like a rebel.

Sera's family had bookshelves with *The Brothers Karamazov* and *House of Mirth* shoved alongside photo books of Paris with titillating titles like *Love on the Left Bank*. Mom kept her Jackie Collins and Harold Robbins novels in a messy pile on her dresser and lent them to her friends when she was finished and never asked for them back. Sera's parents were fat and unpopular, too, but nicer to kids than any of the popular people I knew. They ate ice cream: there were always eight kinds in the house. Mom never had anything in our fridge except her unsweetened sun tea, which guests weren't allowed to touch. When Sera slept over, her parents didn't understand to feed her before she came (it must have been inconceivable to her father, the cook, that his *bella figlia mia*, Serafina, would not be greeted at the door with a meatball or a cannoli), so we had to order pizza, if Mom could afford it that week.

Mom stopped going out when she got breast cancer my sophomore year. And although by then she had come to like Sera well enough, remarking constantly on how thin and cute she had become as though she had not seen her in four years, instead of almost every day, once she got sick she began disliking Sera for a different reason. Now Sera was *too* popular—dragging me to parties every weekend, when Mom could see full well, judging by the fact that the phone rarely rang for me unless it was Sera, that I was invited by virtue of our friendship and not on my own merit. Having a daughter in high social demand loses a significant amount of cachet when you are dropping weight and in pain and have lost one of your breasts. When you are sick, you want your children to be hopeless nerds who have nothing better to do than sit at home with you. Mom was jealous, though when I told Sera's mother that in passing, she winced like I'd smacked myself in the face and said, "Mothers shouldn't be jealous of their children's lives," as though Mom wasn't ill and deserving of any special consideration—as though she'd been wanting to say something like that for a long time, even when Mom had firm, perky boobs. After that, I didn't like Sera's parents as well anymore.

My mother assumed Gus was my boyfriend because he took me to fancy places for dinner, like Oprah Winfrey's new restaurant, *Eccentric*, and I never had to bring any money. No variation of my "we're just friends" speech could convince her. I'd been working at Gus's family's cleaners since January, and several times Mom had come in and run into his parents—each time my heart throbbed with horror that she might insinuate something about "our lovesick kids," accompanied by a lewd wink or other horrible sign. Then Gus's father would fire me, and I wasn't entirely certain that if I didn't see Gus at work every day, our relationship would long survive. (Albeit we were both beginning classes at UIC in less than a month, but all Gus's Greek friends would be there too, opting to stay close to their clan—I obsessed: what excuse would we make to even *associate*?) But each time Mom dropped by, she was quiet, almost unrecognizably demure. I'd taken my job to supplement her losses when she started taking so much time off work—maybe she felt shamed, like Gus's parents were giving her charity. Mom was on disability now; I made more money at the cleaners than she did off her checks.

I fell in love with Gus right away. I'd noticed him even before, in the halls at school, but he hung out with the Greek people speaking Greek, and didn't listen to the Violent Femmes or wear black vintage clothing or swallow speed between classes and drink beer out of McDonald's Coke cups. The Greeks were as foreign to us as the Amish, though once I knew them, I realized they only listened to dance music instead of alternative, and wore shiny, tight clothing Sera's crowd considered tacky, and drank mixed drinks at sponsored Greek dances without needing fake IDs. Gus had no qualms about his Americanized Italian girl-employee hanging around his Greek friends, but we had to hide our romance in case they told his father. We never held hands in public or made out by our lockers like some couples. To compensate for the lack of visible drama, I wrote him long, moony letters in class declaring my undying devotion and calling us "star crossed lovers the world aims to keep apart." When he visited Greece after graduation, I sent him a bottle of Chicago rain, and later, my dishwater brown ponytail wrapped in a blue ribbon when I got my hair bobbed to surprise him. Gus acted pleased by my new hairdo, but his brother George said the ponytail was creepy like *Fatal Attraction* and had scared his aunts, who apparently had no qualms about opening their seventeen-year-old nephew's mail.

This had been going on for six months.

You may be wondering what kind of a person Sera was, that she would tell me, her best friend, that my cancer-ridden mother was a slut. You may be assuming that she said it in anger, out of jealousy that she did not have a boyfriend, that she was still a virgin, that I was leaving her behind. And on some level, I guess all of these deductions would be true. But on a more primal level, Sera's motivation had little to do with guys or even teen-chick competition. She purposely upset me so that she could comfort me. She did it because that was what she knew how to do—was what she *did*—and, in retrospect, was why so many people loved her. She was the one who would point out that your boyfriend was probably cheating on you, and then would take your phone calls four times a night and listen to you cry without ever tiring of your idiocy. She would play match-maker between stocky, desperate girls and their hot, football-player crushes, and when things went wrong and the girls got burned, Sera would pick up the pieces. Sera would disguise her voice and call your mother pretending to be a proper adult for whose child you babysat, in an earnest attempt to enable you to go out on Saturday night, and then when the plot was ultimately foiled, she would scheme with you about how to break out of your house and concur that your mother was a bitch prison warden. She would get you high and then nurse you through a bad trip. Sera was everybody's mother, but a Mephistopheles of a mother, homing in on and somehow catering to your darker side and secret fears or desires.

Oh, don't think we weren't on to her. Behind her back—and to her face—we all agreed she was manipulative, controlling. But teenagers are notoriously bad listeners, fickle-hearted, and by and large fairly stupid about the workings of the human mind, or even how to forge a school absence note that actually looks and reads like it was penned by a fifty year old. She was a rare commodity we could not do without, and we did not, really, mind the dramas she stirred up. We liked to be the center of attention, and Sera could make you feel like you were the center of her world—even if it turned out you were one of ten people to call her that night, and you noticed that she rarely called you. Soon she would be majoring in psychology, but she had been our shrink for years, and much later, in therapy myself, I would see that, like all great analysts, she had a certain ruthless immunity to other people's pain, just as a seasoned surgeon fails to gag when slicing through flesh and yellowed, bulbous fat to the blood and guts beneath. She was fascinated by being needed—by other peoples' capacity for need. That was her fix, *her* need, and while I had not really considered the implications of my failing to confide in her about Gus—when being confided in was her prime vocation—I knew that my need for her was crucial to our relationship. She was the rescuer, and I often needed saving: from my mother's stronger will; from the advances of scary asshole boys; from term papers on books I didn't really grasp; from my future without direction. And now from the jaws of my mother's looming death, which truly was inevitable, we all saw. Sera and I had been friends for eight years, and like a married couple, we had our patterns. She would slice open my skin and fat and stir around my guts, and then she would stitch me back together. And I didn't mind, really. My mother had never really been that interested in what went on under my skin—nobody had, even Gus. Her efforts made me feel loved.

"Before my dad opened the restaurant, when he was still tending bar at Cagney's, he said your mother slept with every regular at the bar and used to hit on him all the time. She had no pride, he said. She'd go with married guys just for buying her a drink. I don't want to see you like that with Gus, just because he has money, just because he's all Oh-I'll-Take-You-To-My-Condo-In-Athens or whatever. He'll never admit he's even dating you—he's totally going to marry some tacky Greek bitch with big hair—if he's even *straight*! Can't you see he's just using you?"

And I could. I could. I could have fallen right into her waiting arms.

But here is what happened instead: I became hysterical.

In the middle of the dance floor, while the Violent Femmes intoned, "One, one, one cause you left me," I felt my face crumple into a grimace and whines welled up between my throat glands. This is what I saw: my father, in the dark corner of the bedroom I would later know only as Mom's, a strap around his arm, tapping, tapping. Then, the arm flying back, strap flailing, as he smacked my mother's face. Some memories *are* fake: I know—I've had flashbacks of various grisly accidents I could never have experienced without being killed: cars plummeting off cliffs and the feeling of free-falling, the claustrophobia of chaos in a burning plane. Other memories verge on dream, like lying in my twin bed at night listening to the radio for so long that the top 40s station turned into the religious station, muffled voices from my mother's room, the sound of something pounding the wall rhythmically, the squeaking of an angry bed... I knew.

Once, I'd even intruded. Once, when I was old enough to know what sex was but young enough to still think it could not apply to my mother—once, knowing Sera got to sleep with her parents when she had a bad dream, I stirred in bed, plotting, gathering nerve, then scuttled across the dark kitchen, conscious of the fact that roaches scurried out of my way, still frightened of me after all the years we'd lived side by side. *I had a nightmare*, I would say to my mother, and wait for her to invite me into her wide, white-sheeted bed, rumpled with the smooth cool skin of *her*. I had the nightmare all planned just in case she asked: Satan lived behind my wall and I was going to have to marry him. But outside her door, I hesitated; I was aware of hunger scraping my stomach, but there was no food in the apartment. I had to pee, but I rarely used the bathroom at night because I didn't like the sight of bugs scurrying when I turned on the light and shocked them. "Mom," I whispered, "Mommy."

An arm on my shoulder. I whirled around, terrified, as though one of the roaches had grown to monster size—I yelped. But it was only Tony Guidubaldi, in my mother's striped terry-cloth robe, his hand circling my shoulder blade like a broken wing he hoped he could repair. "Whatssa matter, babe?" he asked. "You have a bad dream? You lookin' for your ma?" But I burst away and ran the few steps back to my room, hopping into my sweat-sticky bed, listening to the caller on the radio say, *I was saved seven years ago but my son...* I waited for my mother to come and find out what was wrong—she must have heard me in the hall—but she never arrived. In the morning, Tony Guidubaldi was gone, and after that Mom started letting me spend weekends with Sera. Her parents took us on long drives to the Michigan Dunes, cruising in their green Nova for quaint coffeeshops in Cherry Valley where one could obtain the world's best apple pie. Years later, I said to my mother, "When you were dating Tony Guidubaldi," and she said, "Don't be crazy. We never dated—he's married. We were just good friends."

There are some memories that come from a kind of archetype of human suffering: the fear of falling; the hopelessness of trapped limbs thrashing everywhere in a dark, confined space; the itching sting of fire. I went through a stage where I loved all the made-for-TV junkie movies, imagining each addict was my father, and maybe, maybe I *have* transposed his image, his strap, his slap, on a picture I saw long ago: just actors playing a part. Not my father. Not my mother's face. There are memories that do not belong to us, no matter how real they seem. But for a week, Tony Guidubaldi's watch sat on my mother's bureau, and the following weekend, it just disappeared. There are memories that will always be ours, no matter how hard we will them to go away.

Sera had chased me to the bathroom, where I was leaning, weeping over a sink like I might throw up. "Emmy," she pleaded, "it's no big deal. So what about your mom—she's not like that anymore. You're not her—for God's sake, you're a *virgin*—"

"I've been screwing Gus for half a year!" I screamed. "We go at it everywhere—parking lots at night, the bathroom at work the minute George goes on an errand, the elevator at UIC after orientation. You have no idea—you don't know anything about me!"

"Oh, you're lying just to piss me off," she said rationally. "You'd never do that. You're totally scared of guys—besides, we made a pact. You *swore*."

"Duh," I said. "I fucking lied."

Even after she'd torn out of the bathroom, I lingered, sniveling and dwelling on my misery. I was just like my mother, who was dying alone at thirty-nine, jobless in a roach-infested apartment we could only afford because she'd boned the landlord for years, along with every other neighborhood asshole. None of them came around now. None of them would probably even show up at her wake, though maybe I'd get it for free if she'd fucked any of the Ragos who owned the funeral parlor. I would spend my college years letting Gus buy me things, shaking my shoulders on dance floors trying to be somebody else while poor George jerked off nights thinking about my tits, and then Gus would marry some Greek girl just like Sera predicted, or maybe he'd come out of the closet someday, but still I'd be kicked to the side of the road as an obstruction to his Athenian pursuit of tight boy ass. I was the world's biggest loser; I would believe anything; the first time I made a move without Sera and look what I did. I was a slut, and my mother was worse than a slut. My mother was already dead.

Back near the bar, Sera and Gus were arguing. I approached them warily, like a tired mother having to break up the public spats of her annoying children one time too many. Gus grabbed my arm when he saw me—he was a lanky, ethereal boy with fine features, too much fashion sense about women's clothing, and a soft, sweet voice. I had never seen him angry before. "How could you tell her about us?" he hissed in my face. "She's the biggest gossip in the whole school. We might as well go have sex in front of my dad!"

Sera pushed his chest. "Who do you think you are, pretty boy, Conan the Barbarian? Let go of her!"

"Mind your own business," Gus whined like a baby. "Don't *you* think *you've* done enough?"

She rolled her eyes. "Don't be a dork. I'm not going to tell anyone. I'm just mad that Emily broke our pact, so now you guys are going to have to make it up to me somehow."

"Like how?" I said. I knew she was up to something, but I wanted it to be over quickly so I could go home. Gus had the car. I had no money, as usual.

"Well, we were supposed to lose our virginity at the same time," Sera said. Then, with a flourish in Gus's direction—"We vowed ages ago. But now I'm going to have to wait till I get to Madison, because there's nobody here in Chicago who I want to sleep with. I'll have to start college a bitter virgin." She laughed—suddenly, she did not sound bitter. "The sooner I get laid, the less likely I am to be angry that Emily is so selfish. Then I'd have a secret to keep, too."

"So go screw George then," I said irritably. "He's totally in lust with you."

"Eeew," Sera said flatly. "I think not. Gus here got all the charm in the family. Gus, by the way, are you gay?"

"Huh?" Gus said.

"Bi, then?"

"Why are you asking me that?"

"Well, I wouldn't want my best friend Emily to get AIDS. If you're bi, I hope you use protection."

Gus stared at me desperately as if for help. My arm felt bruised; I looked away. I wondered if my mother had fallen asleep on the couch watching TV as usual. I wondered what kind of girl goes out partying and losing her panties in the parking lot of her high school while her bald, breastless mother falls asleep to *The Tonight Show*.

"You *are* really cute," Sera said to Gus. I noticed then that she had never become truly pretty—that despite her new, nice figure and smooth hair and post-braces teeth, her face was somehow already old—it lacked the dewy innocence of youth. We all worshipped her for being smarter and braver than the rest of us, but guys feared her for that, too. Brains don't go far towards getting guys in high school. Sera had never had a boyfriend— never even seemed to fool around with anyone we knew all that well. Our guy friends asked her advice about their naïve, girlie-girl girlfriends while Sera collected dust like a spinster aunt. She must have hated us all: normal girls deemed stupid enough to date by the wanna-be studs who were intimidated by her mind. Maybe she had a right.

"Emily and I always share *everything*," she sing-songed. My eyes bugged. I glanced at Gus, but as I'd failed to come to his rescue a moment before, he refused to meet my eyes now. "I don't like to feel left out."

"Come on." Gus laughed. "You're never left out of anything. You know everything about everyone. What do you care what Emily does with a guy like me? I thought I was, like, totally beneath you."

"Well if Emily thinks you're so great, maybe I should reconsider. She's a very smart girl, you know."

Gus didn't even turn in my direction at this compliment—if that was what it was. His body leaned in closer to Sera, and I thought then: he is either totally *not* gay, or he is way smarter than I thought. Brighter than I was, apparently. Gus's laugh was suddenly throaty; I turned away, speechless. Maybe Sera would not really go through with it—maybe she was only trying to show me what a dog Gus was—how he'd jump at the chance to put his dick in any hole, even right in front of me. I was convinced. How could I let her know? How could I beg her, right in front of him, not to take it too far?

"So if you and Emily *share* something, and it's both of your secret, then you'd keep it together and not tell anybody else, right?" His eyes were seductive—never, even in the moments before climaxing, did he look at me that way. Even under the stars, on the beach in Freeport where I lost my virginity, his eyes had been confused, ambivalent, worried. I remembered how the first time we'd tried to put a condom on his half-mast penis, it kept popping off and flying around the room, and how we chased it, naked at the shabby Tip Top motel on Lincoln, time and time again, until his erection was lost and the condom was dry, so we just watched videos for a couple of hours and then went home. I did not know *that* boy could become this man. Always, I had imagined us as partners in crime: children throwing rocks at old ladies' windows, wild but harmless. I couldn't pretend I hadn't known Sera was capable of treachery, but Gus... Maybe this was why Sera would win—would always win. I did not understand people; I looked at surfaces; I believed what I wanted to believe: in a grown-up mother who would invite me into her safe bed, in Charlie's Angels protecting me from behind my wall. Sera believed in turning human need to her advantage. And need would always win out.

I walked out of the bar.

George was leaning against the brick wall of the building, smoking a cigarette. I had never seen him smoke. His dark eyes were in the shadow of the neon sign; he looked like a gothic vampire, or a detective in a 1940s film. His gaze flicked lazily over me, then back towards the distance, as though he were trying to figure out where he was supposed to be instead of here.

"Do you have any money for a cab?" I asked him.

He shrugged. "I'll take you."

"What about Gus and Sera?"

"Gus has money for a cab. You don't. Either way, my family pays for the cab. So I'll take you."

I followed him to the car. But once inside, he drove towards the cleaners, and I was confused. George lived above the cleaners, and Gus and his parents lived in the building next door. I'd crashed at George's on numerous occasions, on the couch, when it was really late, or I was too drunk to go home. But it was only midnight, and all the drama had sobered me. I said, "I don't think Gus expects me to come back here or anything. I was planning to just go home."

"It's easier this way," he said. "We'll take you back in the morning."

I didn't know what to do. I felt dangerously near crying again, but George was not the sort of person one easily cried around—it was obvious he would think me frivolous and immature, and he might even mock me. I chewed on the inside of my mouth and ventured, "Um, Gus and I kind of had an argument."

"Yeah, I know. My brother's a spoiled asshole."

I gulped.

He took me to his apartment. I was not so clueless as not to consider that he might be trying to get me into bed on the strength of my anger at his brother. But he just handed me a glass of water and left me in the living room, heading to his own bedroom without any attempt at friendly conversation, which was typical. Normally, Gus smuggled me over some blankets and a pillow when I stayed the night, but George hadn't offered. The couch was covered in plastic, and would be uncomfortable without a sheet over it—I curled up on the floor with a sofa pillow and a stiff afghan. Horizontal, my drunkenness returned; the room spun a little. Maybe I was just plowed, and that was why I had reacted so strongly to Sera's comments about Mom. After all, she wasn't saying anything I didn't already know on some level. Maybe I was even drunk enough to have misinterpreted what was going on between Sera and Gus: maybe they were only fucking with me. Maybe Gus would turn up later and spoon me in his arms and say he and Sera had taken separate cabs. Maybe Sera would call my house in the morning and, in her Noel Coward accent, accuse, "Can't you take a bloody joke?"

I *couldn't* take a joke. That had always been a shortcoming of mine. This reassured me as I lulled into a hazy, drunken sleep.

In truth, I must have passed out. I only came to when he tried to enter me. Then my body screamed awake, squirming, jerking in protest, but George's heavy arms, hot from contact and rage and want, bore down upon my bones. He used one hand to guide his rigid penis in, the other arm bent across my chest and bearing all his weight so I gasped for air, my arms flailing like dying snakes, unable to strike. His knees ground into my thighs, holding them apart. Once he was up me, he pushed himself onto both arms, grappling with me briefly as I struck at him, but soon my wrists were in his hands, gripped tight and pushed into the plush carpeting while he pumped into me and I shrieked, then begged, then finally murmured listlessly, "Stop, no." He, too, had been drinking, so his act was perhaps neither as satisfying nor as quick as he'd intended. Near the end he started muttering frantically, "Shit, shit, come *on!*" By the time he climaxed, I was sobbing in pain.

The spasms of the climax seemed to reassure him. "I'll stand up to my father," he groaned into my neck as they shook him. "Forget about Gus, he's a pussy. I have more money than he does anyway. Ahhh, you feel so warm."

I did not bolt for the door when he let go of my wrists, when he rolled off my throbbing legs. My skirt and tights were around my ankles in an indecipherable tangle, my shirt pushed up to my chin, breasts hanging out of my bra so the wires stabbed my tender skin. Semen leaked onto the afghan his mother had made. The clock on the side table indicated that almost four hours had transpired since we'd arrived here and I'd first passed out. Had he slept too, or spent that time watching me, fantasizing, planning?

George fell asleep on the floor, clutching me. It surprised me, more than anything, that he had not invited me to his bed, so clear was it that this rape had, in his mind, heralded in our new romantic relationship. He and Sera and Gus had played a hand of cards, and with a quick reshuffling I was now his. I wept silently while my body went numb and slick under his sweating arm. I did not move until daylight made my nudity unbearable, and I scurried to the bathroom to wash up and rearrange my clothes.

When I re-entered the room, George was sitting up. He offered me orange juice and I took it and drank it without speaking. While he drove me home, he was silent as usual, but before I got out of the car he said, "We'll go to a movie and dinner on Friday—Gus and Sera can accompany us if you like. Think of a restaurant you want to try...but none of that raw fish or Ethiopian mush you girls like."

I did not slam the door.

Approaching my front door under George's gaze, if I thought anything it was, *I always knew this would happen*. Not *him*, not last night's exact scenario, but that prickly sensation on the back of my neck when I found myself in a parking lot alone after dark, or in the deserted restroom of an office building, or when a strange man walked behind me on the street. My fear was the ancient archetype for all women: the knowledge, intrinsic in our flesh, that we can be violated at any time. Now it had happened. It did not occur to me, not once, to call the police—to tell anyone at all. While it would be wrong to say I felt anything resembling *relief*, it might be accurate to say that, finally, I could stop waiting.

From now on my life would exist, like my mother's, *on the other side*.

In the living room, Mom was still asleep under our own afghan, which was store-bought and light and worn from years of use. The TV was off. I sat down at her feet; her toenails were painted seashell pink, but the polish was peeling, her nails growing out. She had several purple splotches on her legs—she bruised easily now. Her head was wrapped in the turban she wore at home; she did not take it off except to shower. Although I was her daughter, and we had lived in this house alone together forever, we were not symbiotic enough that she was comfortable showing me her bald head. Whenever I saw it by accident, I felt a queasy horror akin to remembering my father shooting up, or seeing Tony Guidubaldi's bare feet in our roach infested hall that by rights belonged to him.

I touched my mother's leg, and she opened her eyes and looked at me, but not with any joy at seeing my face, or worry at the expression of pain I wore. Her eyes had gone blank a long time ago. Or maybe I didn't wear any expression of pain, anyway. Maybe my eyes were blank, too. Then, abruptly, below her dead eyes, she smiled.

And suddenly, I could not imagine why I had been so angry at Sera for what she'd said about my mother's past. The clarity of that fury drained from me, and I couldn't remember what was so bad—so inexcusably shameful—about being the neighborhood slut, anyway. With an intensity so rough it doubled me over, I missed the long-past squeaking of my mother's bed, the muffled, complicit adult laughter that excluded me, that rhythmic pounding on the wall our bedrooms shared—the lullaby of my youth. I longed for those days when my mother was still invincible, when I was proud of her for not being like me, but like those brazen girls on the corner who owned our small world. I wanted more than anything to escape the brutal, glaring truths of adulthood: that I never liked those girls, with their gang member boyfriends. That had we grown up together, my mother and I would not have been friends. That my mother never knew me; Sera was the one who understood. That they had both betrayed me. And that I had betrayed them too, with my secrets, my desertion, didn't help. I was alone. Mothers die. College, with neither my best friend nor my first love, loomed.

"Did Sera call?" I asked, though it was only eight in the morning. Before Mom could answer, I blurted, "You know what? I don't think we should answer the phone today. Let's just spend some time together, you and me. Let's not talk to anyone else."

"But what if your boyfriend calls, hon?" Mom said groggily. "It's Saturday. Isn't he gonna want to take you out?" She closed her eyes. I wanted to shout: *Don't!*

There is still one secret Sera never learned. One summer afternoon when we were eleven, on the hottest day of the year, I chose to accompany Mom on the bus to pick out linoleum rather than go with Sera's family to the beach. I told Sera's parents that Mom was dragging me against my will, but the truth was I wouldn't have traded that day for all the cool breezes along Lake Michigan—that I wouldn't trade it now for all the romance of the Aegean Sea. I went because Mom *invited* me. She so rarely invited me. I wore my best, sparkling white jean shorts, like on a date. Sera would have thought I was nuts, but when Mom took me to lunch afterwards, I was too excited to eat, full on nothing but the anticipation of our every happiness.

A Good Plan

Joan Frank

Panting, scanning the linked cars waiting dusty and dumb, I find the numerical zone matching what's printed on our tickets, and yell back to my husband: *We're here.*

The Gare de Lyon is freezing: everything's freezing this slate-colored January morning. Air's filled with car exhaust; with the cold wet rust scent of damp tracks; cigarette smoke, steam from coffee, bread, perfumes. And the din: screeching brakes, shouting crowds, *bongs* of announced arrivals and departures, recorded instructions in musical French, blurred and incomprehensible. We've dragged our giant cases through brown slush. With only minutes to board we've goose-stepped down the long walk, hauled ourselves up and in. I've stalked the aisle to find our seats while my husband struggles to shove the cases into storage between the carriages.

I think I've found our seats. But I can't be certain because a middle-aged man, standing in the seats behind ours, has hung his sweater over the identifying numbers. He rises and, with a glare of distaste at me, collects his sweater.

A girl (I say girl because that is how she will sound when she speaks) is seated beside him at the window, directly behind me. She is vaguely pretty: dyed black hair, a pale, distracted face notably younger than the man's. And the man is notably homely— but these impressions bounce away, vague and unheeded except for the sourness still draping the air from the man's disapproving gaze. *We must appear uncouth to him*, I think—*our breathlessness, our sweaty efforts.* But there's no helping that just now.

Paris to Turin. The car gives a welcome refuge against the bitterness outside, the shocking, burning cold. We arrange ourselves, our coats; we talk, drink water, look out the window. As the train climbs through the Alps the air turns blue and misted and the snow falls faster at a slant, covering the fields we know will, later in the year, glow sweet green. As if in a film's backdrop, the snow drives sideways in lacy flakes; they thicken and intensify, and the landscape—mountainscape—mounds up whiter and whiter.

The sky is low, solid gray.

Behind us, the man has begun speaking to the girl. His voice carries forward and we have no choice but to hear. The man speaks American English. The girl answers with a subtle accent; it might be Russian. Then their chat wanes as they listen to music from a shared device. I can hear the music from the girl's earphones as if from inside a pillbox: "Volare" and "New York, New York" and "Give Your Love to Me," over and over.

The girl makes soft noises marking the music: "ta ta, ta *da*; ta ta, ta *da*."

After a time the man tells her: I don't feel like listening anymore. She makes no reply but continues to listen alone in apparent contentment, whispering ta-*da*'s.

Then the man speaks into his cellphone in Italian. He speaks with a decent accent, and broad assurance. *Si, si*, he says, drawing out the long *eee* of the word as if to mean, *Absolutely*. He asks a question or two. He seems to be the boss of a big company or perhaps a big school, and the person reporting to him on the phone seems to be itemizing various arrangements.

Perhaps the man's company makes perfume. Perhaps it is based in Italy. Perhaps it is clothing his company makes. Maybe the girl is one of its models.

After he hangs up he declares to the girl: They all do everything I want.

A pause. Then she answers evenly:

That is because you are smart.

The train has now crossed the Italian border, and the passport control people have patrolled the aisles, glanced at documents, and gone. The man gives a sudden snorty chuckle, a giggle.

Funny, he says to the girl.

Yes? she answers.

We travel all the way to Italy, he says. And when we get here, it's snowing.

Ah, she answers, uncomprehending. (Not much about how that is funny has reached me, either.)

Then the man's voice becomes a theatrical whisper:

Stay at home and have sex all day, he says.

A silence follows like a struck gong.

In it, I can detect—with every atom of femaleness in me—a furious amount of calculation.

The girl then speaks carefully:

"A good plan."

She says the words as if someone is pinching her very, very hard.

The train pushes past a series of clifftop castles, Tuscan colors flushed with mango light against the snow. Sentinels.

Everyone is staring at the castles. Several passengers murmur in appreciation.

We could take a drive up there tomorrow, I hear the man tell the girl.

Too cold, the girl answers at once.

We could wait until later in the day, the man offers. Have lunch up there.

Silence.

We'll have to figure out, he adds after a moment, what you're going to wear.

At this my husband glances at me, then away.

We've been married many years. We have made what we believe to be a good life, a fair life. But the car feels darker; something ancient has entered the air.

The man keeps trying. His words try to find a way in. The girl's answers bar entry while also striving—with the concentration of a surgeon—to sound technically agreeable, even conspiratorial, possibly festive. It is a masterful effort, like fencing or chess, sublimely calibrated, and it scores my heart like claws.

When the train at last stops at Torino we watch the man move past us to the front of the car to fetch their luggage. He moves alone: the girl is not expected to help. As he passes before us and back again I notice that his hair is graying all over, that his features are in fact homely—and that his rear end, alas, is disproportionately large. His face half-smiles to itself: eager, convinced of its own story in that blind, soaring interval; the heft of its plans like heavy gold coins in the hand. And when the girl finally rises to disembark with the man my glimpse of her is quick: her hair bottle black, her face wary, underslept, her coat and boots good, but worn.

Perhaps my sadness is misdirected.

It may not be that she is indentured—by hunger, by an empty wallet, by slammed doors. She may not be negotiating each moment's precious distance before she can hold off the inevitable no longer—after which the minuet repeats, each round of it offering its small chance to buy extra time before being forced, once more, to touch him.

Perhaps she will even punish him in ways we can't wish to know—ways that leave no visible marks.

Or not.

Maybe neither will recollect these hours and weeks when, years from now in separate lives, each glances backward. Maybe too much else will have accosted them in the interim struggle, avalanched them, to command remembering.

The two step out into the world that made them.

Lil

Melissa Fraterrigo

We were not so different, Lil and I. She hired me to help clean her apartment after her surgery, around the same time I was getting to know the Turners. Back then she was always complaining about pain in the missing part of her leg. Everything aches, Lil said, her body slipping over the seat of her chair, urging me to open the package of cookies she could no longer eat. That's what I thought she liked best: to buy me things she craved, as if by watching me nibble on Oreos the taste might somehow transfer to her own mouth.

In school, I pretended to do my homework, but really I just propped a textbook over my sketchpad and drew. I'd invented a whole family by then: the Turners. Dad was a trim man with a beard and briefcase, Mom wore floral blouses and the children were Theodore and Lena. I'd filled a whole notebook of images of the Turners doing everyday things: swimming in the pool on a Saturday afternoon, sharing a 4th of July picnic, opening presents on Christmas morning. Drawing them delighted me unlike anything else, and sometimes, after I'd finished my work cleaning up after Lil, I'd take out my sketchpad and draw. The first time she asked to see my work my palms had sweated and when she let out a low whistle, I felt as if I'd been baptized, as if my presence only became real in that moment.

I helped Lil after school, finally away from the taunts of the other kids or worse, their quiet stares. There was another girl like me who came during the day, only she and Lil ran errands and did a few things outside the apartment. I'd see Lil's wheelchair along the wall and I'd think there was no way I could take Lil out. Not for double what she paid. Maybe triple. Still, it was what Lil wanted: for me to take her downtown. For us to get our nails done or eat at the new banquet hall. Supposed to have great rolls, she'd say. I wouldn't respond. Then: you remind me of myself, she'd say, and my skin would get all prickly. She was the last person I hoped to become.

When dinners with my parents seemed at their worst and the heat of their eyes burned long after I left the table, I'd turn to the Turners. They lived in a four-bedroom colonial with an open floor plan, similar to what I'd seen in my mother's magazines. They had a backyard swing set for Lena, who was five, and Theodore, who was nine, also liked to play on it, only he twisted the swings around the frame so Lena couldn't use them. These were things boys did.

As I stacked Lil's magazines and cleaned the area around her bird Budgie's cage I planned my drawings. Seed peppered the back of the couch, around the toaster, even in the bathroom where she kept her toothbrush.

"Need to keep the bird in the cage, Lil," I'd say.

She'd sigh. "Budgie."

"Need to keep Budgie in the cage." I'd make a show of closing the door on his cage. Lil would turn the TV on then, pout, and I would finally get on with my work, the whole time thinking about the Turners. The kids would be getting off the bus, Lena swinging her book bag, Theodore running ahead to make plans with a boy who lived one street over. I dusted the window ledges, wiped the counters, took the sheets off her bed and started a load in the washer down the hall. I threw my own clothes in piles on the floor of my room at home, but I liked putting Lil's apartment in order.

After her show went to commercial she'd be ready to talk again. "When I was your age I had a string of boyfriends. My mom nearly kept a list of them on the fridge so she didn't lose track." Lil jutted her chin, smoothed her hair. "Girl, get me my makeup."

I'd bring the flowered bag with that melty soft cotton and she'd unzip it and take out a little mirror, put on some lipstick. She'd smack her lips together, the pink as bright as a fluorescent notepad. "That's nice, right?"

"You look fine, Miss Lil."

"Hush now. Just Lil. I ain't your momma. We're friends, sugar. Now go on. You've done enough." Lil would clap her hands and the heft of her arms wagged out the sleeves of her top. "We got you some good stuff today."

I'd go to the cabinet where Lil and her daytime girl had made a shelf for me.

"You know you're my favorite," she'd say.

Cream pies and sugar cereals and the like. Potato chips. "Pick something nice, now. Come on."

I'd grab whatever was closest. Never liked food the way some people do, and then I'd sit on the little ottoman in front of Lil, right by the stump of her leg. She'd have this gigantic smile on her face and it would get even bigger as I tore into whatever treat I'd chosen. I munched on a chocolate covered graham cracker, the crumbs always seeming more crumbly because of the fact she was watching me. "Don't be shy, girl. How is it?"

"Delicious."

"Oh good." And Lil, who'd lost a leg to diabetes and always seemed in danger of losing the other one, rocked back and forth.

"What I wouldn't do," she said. "Corn pops and chocolate chip cookies. My mom's coconut custard pie. Mmhmm."

Most days were like this. I'd do a little work at Lil's, she'd urge me to eat junk food, and I'd comply. "If only I could do it all over again," she'd say. "I'd do the homework. I'd get the grades. And I'd eat every treat, Mo. I'd eat it all. Now let me see your pictures."

I'd watch Lil's thick fingers turn the pages of my sketchpad. She'd shake her head back and forth, telling me what she liked best. I listened to her and afterwards I'd get the mail so she could look through the sale papers while I vacuumed. While the other kids were taking piano or tae kwon do, I was helping Lil whose daughter was always sending postcards with tropical vistas, trying to convince Lil to live with her in Florida.

"Do you know what summers are like there? Plus I won't know nobody." She'd let her voice drift off then and I didn't know if I should speak or remain quiet. I told myself I needed the job. My mom had grown up with little and was determined I'd be self-sufficient. She had been the one to find the advertisement on a corkboard outside the grocery store and handed it to me, told me it was time I earned some of my own money. Still, I was failing most of my eighth-grade classes and couldn't imagine things going on like this: high school, then graduation and maybe community college.

My parents were on the cusp of divorcing, my mom railing about my dad some days, throwing all his boxers and old copies of *Car & Driver* into a box one day and then sobbing other days when he was so late for dinner it seemed he might never come home.

When she wasn't vacillating between the two extremes, my mother worked as a pharmacist, filling prescriptions and ringing up pints of ice cream. She never gave the impression that the future was something to look forward to, and my father, when he was around, kept his head tucked inside a book. He liked to read about ancient people and lands as if the past were something he was determined to learn from. When he and my mother were in the same room, air heaved with tension.

She blamed him for the smallness of our lives: the little house with the overgrown crabgrass, burnt dinners and once-a-year vacations to a rented cabin near a brown lake when what she wanted was for our life to look like it did in the glossy magazines she brought back from the drugstore. Sometimes my father tried. One birthday he gave her a gold watch with a diamond chip on the second hand. She cried when she opened the box and kissed him on the lips.

Early on I learned not to refuse a gift.

Every dinner with my parents was an exercise in restraint as they struggled to speak humanely to each other. Most of the time it was easier for them to direct their disdain toward me: my thin hair and chewed fingernails—ordinariness.

"Did you read the article about the girl who won this year's spelling bee?" Mom asked. "She was only ten."

"Probably had tutors and the like," said my dad, eager to take anything magical and make it less so. My mom aimed to soar in the sky and he was content to amble sidewalks. Their disagreements extended to me as well. My mom wanted me to do more, be more, while my dad thought I'd find my way eventually.

After a particularly long dinner, I returned to my room where I decided to give the Turners a neighbor. He was a single bachelor who liked to help Mr. Turner with projects and was handy in a way Mr. Turner was not. When Mrs. Turner invited him over for a cookout, he ate two of everything and complimented her cooking. I named him Brandon for a boy in my class that everyone had a crush on. Only my Brandon had beautiful hands that could wield hammers and wrenches, a flower garden that buzzed with butterflies and a box of cherry Popsicles in his freezer for the neighborhood kids.

As I drew, details of Brandon's life came into sharp focus— the books at his bedside table, the print of the wallpaper in his hallway, the old Coke bottles he collected and displayed on a shelf near his kitchen.

I was working on a sketch of Brandon's bulldog when my mother came into my room. She stood over my shoulder and watched me draw. I could tell by her silence that she'd been crying, but in my room I felt impervious to her needs. "How's Mrs. Lillian?" she asked.

"Fine."

"Is it too much to juggle with your homework?"

I said that it wasn't.

"Your grades have to come first," she said.

I stopped my pencil. Her eyes were puffy from crying.

"Do you think I should leave him?" she asked, muffling a strangled sob. "Don't answer that!" She moved over to the window and looked out at our neighbor's siding. "I shouldn't be doing this," she said, and petted my flat hair, then looked down at her hand.

I stayed up for hours that night wallpapering Theodore's room with skulls and crossbones, driven by a head banger's fury.

The kids at school made jokes and pushed my books off my desk, stuffed mean notes in my locker. To this day I don't know why. All I wanted to do was draw and I wasn't interested in their music or video games. But I had purpose at Lil's, so on the day I came in and she introduced me to Mike, I didn't think much of it. He was fixing a leak under the kitchen sink and popped his head out long enough to wave hello and fix his brown eyes on mine. I was momentarily frozen. This Mike looked just like Brandon, the Turners' neighbor, except my Brandon wore khakis and polo shirts. Still, it was an unsettling feeling seeing my drawing in the flesh.

I put my backpack in its usual place by the door and asked Lil how she was feeling. "Not bad, love. Young people like you and Mike make me hopeful. Go on. Get your snack." I had to step over Mike's legs to get to the cabinet and took out a package of Nutter Butters. I felt shy enough with Mike there to get down a plate. As I was doing so, Mike moved his legs and his work boots sloshed side to side like wipers. I ate my cookies next to Lil, and then licked my finger to pick up every crumb from the plate. Afterwards I started cleaning up after Budgie.

"I told him he needed to pick up after himself, but he wouldn't listen," Lil said. I was dusting the table where she stacked her *Reader's Digest*s when Lil grabbed my wrist. "Looky that," she said, fixing the clasp of her hand over my wrist. "I'm starting to think they don't feed you. We're going to have to get you more goodies."

I shrugged. "Guess I'm growing and all that."

"All righty!" announced Mike. He stood upright in the kitchen, brushed his hands on the thighs of his jeans. "Leak should be gone." He was taller than he'd looked when he was stretched out on the floor and he was older, maybe in his early twenties. He had a dimple in his left cheek just like Brandon, the same soft wave in his hair like he had just stepped off a sailboat. Watching him, my hand started to tingle for pencil and paper.

"Now Maureen gets sugar. What am I going to give you?"

He shook his head. "This is what they pay me for." The kitchen looked so small and dingy with him in it, and after he left I filled a bucked of hot water with Mr. Clean and scrubbed the linoleum. "Smells nice," Lil said. I thought so, too.

That night I skipped dinner and in my room, drew Brandon taking his dog for a walk, waving at his neighbors, stopping to let the dog sniff a tree. I knew it was Mike, but I wasn't ready to puzzle out how that had happened.

Mom came into my room, asking if I felt all right. She put a hand to my forehead and I momentarily closed my eyes to the cool of her touch. I thought of forgiving her for everything. "I'm fine. Just a little headache."

"Take a Tylenol."

When she went to peer at my notebook, I put a hand over it. "It's not finished."

She shrugged. "Must be nice to be able to draw, to have your own room with a door, food on the table, clean clothes." Her voice had a sudden harshness to it. I wanted to tell her to get the divorce but I didn't yet know how to speak my mind.

I closed my notebook and stood up. "I'm going to bed."

"I'm so fed up with your father," she said.

I slid off my jeans, turned off the light and got under the blankets. My mother stood there in the dark. I could hear her breathing. "Good night," she finally said, and shut the door behind her.

I didn't tell Lil about my parents or the kids at school, but she seemed to sense it and on the day I received detention for drawing Brandon introducing his girlfriend to the Turners rather than working on math, Lil told me to sit down and patted the armrest of the couch beside her. "I've always said a girl is nothing without a boy. And it's time you get that boy." She went on to tell me the story of her first boyfriend. His name was Johnny Bonner and everyone called him that—both his first and last name. "When he held my hand at the movies I thought I was going to pass out. You see me now, like this, but there was a time I was pretty, like you."

Budgie was securely in his cage, his pencil toes tipped along the swing that hung from the center. It made a squeaking sound that made my skin itch.

"Johnny Bonner took that hand and made it special."

There was a knock at Lil's door that she asked me to get.

I opened the door. Mike stood there with a box of tools. "I'm here for the furnace."

I froze, then caught myself and stepped to the side. His resemblance to Brandon was uncanny. I breathed out of my mouth, tried to regain calmness. Suddenly, calm was the last thing I felt.

I left to get the mail and closed the door behind me, the light spicy scent of Mike's deodorant lingered in the hallway. When I came back inside I saw that the two kitchen chairs were positioned next to each other in front of Lil's chair. Mike was sitting in the one on the left. Lil clapped her hands. "You're back!"

I handed her the sale papers and a few bills but she tossed them onto the couch. She told me to take a seat next to Mike. "This is Johnny Bonner and you're me."

Mike looked sheepish. "I don't have anywhere to be but 12B."

Heat collected in my face.

"We're just play-acting. Just like all those sketches." Lil sat up straighter and her stump pointed at me like a bayonet. I slid onto the seat, tucked my hands between my legs. "Now I'll paint the picture: You've had your eyes on one another for weeks when you ask her to see *Star Wars*. And you've spent hours getting ready." Lil paused. "Go get my bag."

When I came back with it she told me to come closer. I crouched in front of her as she put her lipstick on me. I could hear my mother complaining about germs, but found that with effort, her voice gradually disappeared.

The soft lacquered smell of the lipstick creamed my lips, and Lil had a look of intense concentration as she painted me. Closed blinds shut off the day's brightness, filled the room with a pearly gray. "Now you take her hand."

And my hand, which had drawn countless figures and scenes was suddenly inside Mike's hand.

"Now stroke her arm, Mike. Do it kind."

"I don't know about that, Miss Lil. What if—

"Hush! Do it!" Her voice icy slick.

He touched me, and my skin became alive, hairs springing to attention. "Maureen, you like this boy. More than any other. So you've got to show him. You've got to prove it."

I thought of Brandon, the Turners' neighbor. What was he doing at night? Who was he with when a soft glow seeped onto the evergreens outside his picture window?

I hadn't considered it before, but now I realized my error. I remembered a picture from one of my mother's magazines and turned to Mike. I picked up my hand and wanted to place it on his chest, all my fingers lining up like in the ad, the woman's oval red nails and gold bracelets against the smooth panes of his naked chest, but Mike wore a T-shirt, a few errant hairs springing over the rim of his neck.

I stood and ran into the bathroom, locking the door behind me. I splashed water onto my face and peered at my eyes. They were a flat brown and I blinked, noticed how the dark lashes framed my eyes. I thought of Mrs. Turner and how her hair was always neatly brushed, a smile on her face. I'd never considered the Turners before they moved to their current home next door to their neighbor. At one point it had been only the two of them, maybe watching a movie in the theater.

A whole lifetime began with one gesture.

I sat down on the crocheted toilet seat cover and didn't come out until I heard the apartment door open and shut. "He's gone, Maureen," called Lil. "Now come out of there."

She sighed. I knew she couldn't get out of her chair without assistance.

When I finally left the bathroom, Lil asked me to sit down, said she wanted to talk to me. "What I did wasn't right. But what you're doing isn't right either. Moping around, cleaning up after me. I don't know your parents, but if you were my own daughter I'd teach her to cherish her body, her youth. Someday you'll look like me. Not crippled maybe, but old. You're gonna get old. Understand?"

I said that I did.

That night I showered and lathered everything twice until the bathroom was thick with steam, and then I dressed in clean pajamas. I sat at my desk and drew the Turners as teenagers. They went to school together but it wasn't until he cut her grandmother's lawn and she happened to be outside tending to an injured baby robin she'd found on the sidewalk that they'd talked.

The next time he took my hand, I was ready. The light in the apartment grainy gray. Mike made a noise that sounded like a kitten, something hoping to be petted. His voice deep. "You can't just leave me like that," he said, and before the words registered, he kissed me on the lips. He tasted of cigarettes and chewing gum, and when I went to pull away he grabbed my face and suddenly his tongue wormed inside my mouth. I stood up, wiped my mouth, my lips feeling too loose for my face. "Way to go!" Lil cheered.

Lil dated Johnny Bonner for three months and they made it to second base.

My parents separated that summer and my mom and I moved into an apartment of our own on the other side of town too far from Lil's apartment for me to continue working for her. Mom took on extra shifts at the pharmacy and didn't get home until late at night. I drew, only this time I didn't share the pictures with anyone. When Mike came to our apartment after school, I let him in.

Sunshine

Lynn Freed

They told Grace they'd found her curled into a nest of leaves, that since dawn they'd been following a strange spoor through the bush, and then, just as they'd begun to smell her, there she was, staring up at them through a cloud of iridescent flies.

They peered through the mottled gloom. Flies were clustered on her nose and eyes and mouth, and yet she didn't move, didn't even blink. "It's dead," said one of them, stretching out a stick to prod her.

That's when she sprang, scattering the flies and baring all her teeth in a dreadful high-pitched screech. They leapt back, reaching for their knives. She was up on her haunches now, biting at the air between them with her jagged teeth. But with the leaves and flies swirling, and her furious, wild hair, it took some time before they understood that it was a girl raging before them, just a girl.

"Hau!" they whispered, and they lowered their knives. She was skinny as a stick – filthy and naked, and the nest smelled foul. One of the men dug into his pocket for some nuts. "Mê," he said, holding them out to her, "Mê."

She lifted her chin, trying to sniff at the air. But her nose was swollen and bloody, one arm hung limp at her side.

"It will be easy to catch her," the older man said. "How do we know the Master won't pay? Even half?"

•••

Julian de Jong stormed out into the midday sun. "What on earth's the matter out here, Grace?" he said. "Why've you locked the dogs away?"

One of the men held the girl up, the other lifted her hair so that the Master could see her face.

"They found her in the bush, Master," Grace said, not looking up. She never wanted to see the girls when they were brought in. "They say if they put her back, maybe the jackals will get her."

The girl writhed and twisted to free herself from the grasp of the men. She bared her teeth, screeching pitifully. All the way up the hill, she had screeched and struggled like this, and all the way baboons had come barking after her.

de Jong stepped out into the yard and the men dropped their eyes courteously. Everyone knew he was not to be looked at when he was inspecting a girl, even an ugly one like this, even their own daughters. The girl stopped her squirming when he walked up, as if she, too, knew what was good for her. She stared at him as he questioned the men, breathing lightly through her mouth like a dog.

He put his monocle to his eye, and, for several minutes, examined the girl in silence. And then, at last, he stood up and said, "Grace, clean the creature up. Here," he said to the men, digging around in his pocket for change. "Take this and divide it between you."

•••

"Bring me the scissors!" Grace said to Beauty. "Bring me the Dettol!"

Beauty held the girl down while Grace took the scissors to her hair. "Ag!" she said, handing the tangle of hair and grass and blood to the garden boy. "Burn that," she said. "And bring me the blade for shaving. And the big tin bath."

By the time the bath was filled with hot water, the girl was almost bald, her scalp as pale as dough, and bleeding here and there from the blade. When they tried to lift her in, she struggled even more, twisting and thrashing and working one leg free so that she slashed at the flesh of the Grace's arm with a toenail.

"Be *still*, you devil!" Grace cried, giving her a hard slap on the flesh of her buttock. "You want to go back to the bush? You want the jackals to get you?"

But the creature would not be still. By the time she was clean, the kitchen floor was awash with dirty water and she was cowering against the side of the bath, shivering, the teeth chattering. Now that she was clean, they could see that the nose and arm had been badly broken, and that the skin was sallow where the sun had not caught it. It was covered in scratches – some old, some new – and her hands and feet were callused as hooves.

"He'll send her back after all this trouble," Beauty said. She was standing in the kitchen doorway with an armful of clothes. They were the same clothes each time, flimsy things that the girls loved to wear. "They will only be spoiled," she said. "It's a big shame." She put them on the kitchen table.

Grace pulled a small chemise out of the pile. She didn't understand these clothes, she hadn't understood them when she'd had to wear them herself. "Hold up her arms," she said to Beauty.

But it was hopeless. One by one, the clothes were tried, torn, bitten, abandoned. The best Grace could do was to pin a dish cloth onto the girl as tightly as she could. And then once it was on, the creature only squatted on her haunches like a monkey and clawed at the cloth with her good hand, drawing blood in her madness to have it off.

"It's too cruel," said Grace. "Let's take it off."

And so the girl was carried onto the verandah, naked and bald, to be presented to the man who would decide what would become of her.

•••

Over the years, there had been rumours in the local villages of children living with baboons in the forest – of children snatched by baboons if you left them outside unguarded. Some children the baboons ate, the rumour went, some they kept for themselves. But only the old women ever believed this.

"Look again," Julian de Jong said to the local administrator. "See if anyone reported a baby missing – six or seven years ago, white, half-breed, anything you can find. I don't want any trouble later."

But no one had reported such a thing, not in the whole province. No one would challenge his claim.

"She could have been thrown away as a newborn and left for dead," said Doctor McKenzie, leaning over to examine the arm. "Some desperate teenager, who knows? I suppose it's not out of the question that baboons could have taken her up. But it hardly seems plausible, does it? Mind you, these fractures could very well be the result of a fall from a tree. She could have grown too big, I suppose. And she's malnourished, which would make her prone to fractures. Anyway," he said, straightening up. "There it is, and something needs to be done about the teeth. Don't mind telling you, old boy, I'm glad *I'm* not the dentist. Oh, and here – don't leave without the worm powder. Sure you're up for this one, Julian?"

•••

The first night, de Jong had Grace lock the girl into the storeroom in the servants' quarters. But all through the night, the creature screeched and wailed, keeping the servants awake. The next morning they found that the sling on her arm had been bitten away, the bandage torn from her nose. Even her callused hands and feet were bloodied and raw from trying to climb to the small, barred window above the door.

"It's cruel to lock her in there, Master," said Grace. "She's like an animal. We must train her like a dog."

de Jong looked at the girl. All night she had visited him in dreams – more like presences, really, than dreams – but, when he woke up, he could still put no face to the creature. Usually he knew just what he had. At first they'd cry and beg to be sent home. Sometimes it would go on for weeks, and then he'd have to punish them. But in the end Grace always managed to have them ready for him, cleaned and oiled and docile.

If there was a principle that drove Julian de Jong, it was never to obscure his motives. And so, from the outset, there'd never been a question of theft. He was doing the girls a favor, everyone knew that, even their families. How else could it be that old McIntyre the missionary had never got any of them to talk? They'd just shake their heads when he came calling, press their lips together. They knew that when he was finished with them, the girls would fetch a decent bride price regardless. There was the money, of course, but there were other things, too, things they'd learned them from Grace – how to lay the table and mend the sheets, and sometimes even how to make a pudding or a soup. And so, when he finally sent them home, they seemed not to know where they'd rather be. And who was the worse for it then?

He stretched out his hand to touch the rough skin of the creature's cheek. He wanted to stroke it as he would stroke one of the others when she was new, for the pleasure of the life under his hand – grateful, warm, blameless. But just as his fingers came near her, she whipped her head around and tore at the flesh of his thumb with her teeth.

"Good God!" he cried, watching the blood well into the wound. He grasped the wrist tightly with his other hand as if to restrain it from grabbing her by the throat. And all the while, she was staring at him, panting, waiting, ready.

Grace lowered her eyes. She had seen him take the riding crop to a girl for staring. She had seen him take the crop to a girl for doing nothing at all.

"I'll call Beauty to fetch the Gentian, Master," she said quickly.

He turned then, as if he had forgotten she was there. A breeze was up, playing with his frizzy grey hair. But there was nothing playful in his face, she knew. It was flushed with fury, ready for the Lord knew what.

"Grace," he said, "I want you to tell the rest of them that no hand is to be laid upon this girl, not even if she bites. You will treat her like any of the others. Do you hear me?"

"Yes, Master."

•••

"de Jong," McKenzie said, smoothing down the last of the plaster of Paris. "She will need to be restrained to a board if this is to do any good. And I'll have to fashion a bucket collar so that she can't get at the nose. No one come forward to claim her?"

"No one."

"Well, the word is out, you know. The papers are bound to dig it up sooner or later."

"Let them dig. I have Dunlop's word he'll fix things. Anyway, who'd want her? She's an animal – just look what she did to my hand this morning."

McKenzie took the hand and turned it over. "It'll need a stitch," he said. "And we should test her for rabies. Here, keep still."

Grace took the girl to the chair in the corner. She held her there by the wrists, securing the girl's hips between her own copious thighs. But still the girl strained forward, as if she wanted another go at de Jong's hand.

"How long till the bones knit?" de Jong said.

"Bring her back in four weeks, and we'll take a look."

●●●

For four weeks, the girl was kept strapped to a board on the sleeping porch of the upstairs verandah. There Grace fed and cleaned her, and there, every night, de Jong himself slept in the bed next to hers, talking softly to her, telling her things he wouldn't have told the others. The hot season was beginning to die down, but when he tried covering her with his knee rug, she gasped and gagged, straining against the straps that held her head in place. So he took it off again.

After a while, he began to sit at the edge of her bed, and then place a hand on her forehead, almost covering her eyes. He'd hold it there until she stopped struggling, and, when she did, he'd run his fingers around the coil of an ear and under her jaw, down into the curve of her neck and shoulders. And then, if she was quiet, he'd feed her a piece of raw liver, which she loved best of all.

And so, soon he had her suffering his touch without struggling. She would lie still, staring at him around the plaster on her nose. Once, as his hand slipped itself over her rump, she even closed her eyes and fell asleep, he could hear her breathing settle. But when he stood up to leave, she was instantly awake again, following him with her eyes through the fading light to his own bed.

As the fourth week approached, de Jong had a cage built and placed at the back of the sleeping porch. Inside, Grace placed a tin mug and bowl, his knee rug and a driving glove that had lost its pair. The girl was to be lifted so that she could see every stage of the preparations, and Grace was to hold the bowl for her to sniff before she put it inside, and then the rug, and then the glove.

"Master," Grace said. "Maybe she's not so wild now. Maybe we can let her walk for herself when the arm is better."

But the minute the plaster was off and the girl was given the freedom of the cage, she began to rage and screech again as if she had just been caught. With both arms growing stronger, she began to climb and swing and leap as well. She bit and tore at the blanket until it lay in shreds on the floor of the cage. The glove she examined carefully, turning it this way and that way, and then testing it with her teeth. The teeth themselves had been drilled and cleaned before the plaster came off. But they were still brown, and a few had been pulled out, giving her an even wilder look.

No one could work out how old she really was. Certainly, she was the size of most of the girls they brought to him. But the dentist seemed to think she was a bit older, which made the whole thing a little more urgent. All night and much of the day, de Jong stayed up there, talking softly to her. The servants watched and listened. It was the voice that he used for the dogs, and for the girls when they were first brought in. Never for anyone else. After a while even the girl herself seemed to listen. She would stare at him through the bars of the cage, frowning her baboon frown. And then he would pour some water into her mug, showing her how to drink it without lapping.

Over the weeks, she became quiet for longer and longer stretches of time. Even when de Jong went away and Grace came up to sit with her, she would wait quietly for her water, for her food. It was Grace herself who found a way to stop the girl tearing up the newspaper that was placed there day after day for her mess. And then one day, when the girl messed on it by chance, Grace began to sing. "You are my sunshine," warbling in her high-pitched vibrato, and the girl cocked her head like a bird, this way and that way. She ran to the bars and hung on, waiting for more. But Grace just waited too. And the next time the girl messed on the newspaper, she sang the song again, adding a line or two. And so, with singing, Grace managed to coax the creature into a pair of pants and a vest, and by the time de Jong returned, she'd learned how to pull them off and put them on herself.

"Master," Grace said, "maybe we can unlock the dogs now."

And so the dogs were led one by one to the cage, ears back, straining at the leash. When the girl heard them coming, she ran wildly for the far corner of the cage, upsetting the bowl, climbing the bars and hanging there, screeching with all her teeth. The dog itself would jump up, wagging, barking wildly, only to be scolded, corrected, made to sit and stay.

Day after day the ritual was repeated until dog and girl could stare at each other without fright. After a while, de Jong could trust the dogs to approach the cage unleashed. And then, at last, when the girl was ready to be taken out, the dogs ran beside her without incident.

"Master," Grace said, "I can't make her stand straight like you said. She still wants to bend over like a baboon. I think she was living with the baboons over there. I think she can still be like them."

de Jong smiled down at the girl. Thick black curls were beginning to cover her head. And her face was beginning to reveal itself, the nose long and straight, a high forehead, small ears, olive skin and the wide black eyes of a gypsy. Considering only the head, she could be any child, any dark, silent girl, no breasts yet, no body hair either. If she still stooped, what difference would it make? She was ready, baboons or no baboons, he could see it in the way she looked at him. It was Grace who was trying to hold her back for some reason.

"You'll bring her to me tomorrow evening," he said. "The usual hour."

Grace bowed her head. Usually, she was only too glad to hand a girl over because then she'd have her two weeks off. When she did return, as often as not the girl would be over the first fright of it. So what had come over her this time? "Maybe a few more days?" she said.

He smiled at Grace. It was almost as if she'd known from the start how it would be with this girl. And now that he was taking pride – well, not so much pride in the girl herself as in the things she could do, the way he could make her obey him – now that he was waking each morning to the thought of what he might make the girl do for him next, now came Grace with her suggestions.

"She does not even have a name yet," Grace said.

They were walking down to the river, which the girl always liked to do. Once he'd thought he heard her laugh – laugh or bark, it was hard to tell which. The sun was shining brilliantly on the muddy water, and she'd looked up into his face, her mouth and eyes wide. And then, freeing her hand from his, she'd bounded down the hill with the dogs, down to the water's edge.

"Tomorrow evening. In the atrium. The usual time."

•••

Grace had dressed the girl in a simple silk shift. There was a pool in the middle of the atrium, with a fountain at its centre. Most of the girls couldn't swim, but the pool was shallow, and he'd be sitting in it, naked, waiting for them with his glass of whiskey. The girls themselves always stopped at the sight of him there, the pink shoulders and small grey eyes. And then he'd rise out of the water like a sea monster and they'd make a run for it, every one of them, never mind how much Grace had told them there was no way out.

Men in the village liked to say they'd come to the house one night and cut off his manhood like a paw-paw. But Grace knew it was all talk. Without his money, where would they all be? Where would she be herself? The Master himself knew that, standing there, shameless, before her. But when he had finished with this one, where would she go? Usually, they'd run home with the money, and then, sooner or later, they'd be back at the kitchen door, wanting work. But what about this one? Where *could* she go except back to the baboons?

Quickly, Grace turned and walked out of the atrium.

•••

He held his hand out to the girl, but she didn't take it. She was leaning over the low wall, splashing one hand into the water. He caught it in his own then, and took her under the arms and lifted her in. She didn't struggle, she was used to his lifting her here or there. But this time he was lifting her dress off her, too, throwing it aside. She wasn't wearing any panties, he never wanted them wearing panties when they came to him. So now there was nothing but her smooth, olive skin. He ran his hands down her sides and cupped one around each buttock – small and round and girlish, the rest of the body muscled like a boy's.

She let him coax her down into the water, lapping at it happily. And when he moved one hand between her legs, she just glanced down there through the water with the frown she always wore when Grace tried to show her how to wipe herself after she'd used the toilet. But he was stroking her, prodding into her with a finger so that she jumped away and stared hard at him. And still he came after her, taking her by the arms before she could scramble up onto the fountain. He was pushing her backwards to the side of the pool and his smile was gone, he was holding her arms wide so that he could force his knee between her legs.

Caught like that, she slammed her head wildly then from side to side against the edge of the tiles, shrieking piteously. A trickle of blood ran down her neck, and when at last he had her legs apart and was thrusting himself into her, she was bleeding there, too. He knew from her narrowness that she'd be bleeding properly when he'd finished with her, that her blood would cloud out beautifully into the pool, turning from red to pink. It was the moment he longed for with every new offering, first the front, then the back, and always the mouths open in astonishment like this, the eyes wild and pleading, and for what? For more? More?

By the time he was finished with her and resting his head against the side of the pool, she was moaning. They all moaned like this, and what did they expect? What did this one expect after all these months she'd kept him waiting with her grunts and squawks. He stretched out an arm to grab her neck. Usually that's all it took to shut them up. If it didn't, he'd duck them under the water until they were ready to listen. "Quiet," he'd croon in his deep, soft voice. And if that didn't work, he did it again, and for longer. "Do you hear me now?" he'd whisper. "I said quiet!"

But with this one words were useless. And, just as he was about to push her under, she slipped free, twirling herself into the air, twisting, leaping, springing out of reach until, at last, he had caught her by an arm. But then she only doubled back, sinking her teeth into his wrist, and, when he'd let her go, into an ear, and, at last, as his hands flew to his head, she took his throat between her jaws. And there she hung on like a wild dog, only tightening her bite as he bucked and flailed for air. But the more he struggled the deeper she bit, never loosening her jaws until he was past the pain, past the panic. Only then, only after the last damp gurgling of breath had left him limp, did she rip away the flesh and gristle she'd got hold of, and, gulping it down as she ran, leap out through an open window.

•••

When they came in with the tea things, the whole pool was pink, pinker than they'd ever seen it, even the fountain. At first they'd just stood there, staring at what was left of his throat. But then they remembered the girl, and they ran, one for a kitchen knife, another to lock the doors and windows of the house.

But she never returned. And the generations that followed were inclined to laugh at the whole idea of a baboon girl – of *any* girl killing that demon like a leopard or a lion. They were inclined to doubt the demon himself as well. Surely someone would have reported him to the authorities, they said? Surely one of his girls would have told her story to the papers?

Preferences

Amina Gautier

Jamie wakes in a bed that is not her own. It is Mikhail's bed and Mikhail's cramped apartment and tonight is the first night she has ever heard of this name attached to someone young, attractive and American rather than old, political, and Russian. Mikhail is a grad student at her university, but he is not her T.A. and they are not on-campus, so it is all right.

He has taken her to his place in one of the nearby towns whose name she always forgets. It is either Mountain View or Menlo Park, depending on which way they headed on El Camino.

Drinks in his apartment, seated on his floor near his couch, her back against his chest, his legs on either side of hers, comfortable. Mikhail says he went to the party "on a lark" and she finds the phrase expressive, charming. Jamie is a smart girl, capable of appreciating irony.

Mikhail has no television. Planks of wood balanced on cinder blocks serve as bookshelves. There are more books than shelves to hold them. Books are stacked haphazardly atop each other, splayed open. More than a few are upside down. His many books are haggard with wear and tear. Even from her seat on the floor, she can see the violence that's been done to them. She thought a grad student would have been gentler.

He offers her a back rub.

How easy and innocent it all begins. Thumbs kneading shoulders, pads of flesh digging into skin. A simple whispered question, "Wanna come with me to the back room?"

The moment is so similar to the one earlier in the evening when—her back braced against the wall and his hands nestled in the back pockets of her jeans—Mikhail nuzzled her and said, "Do you want go somewhere and maybe have a drink or two?"

She appreciates the way he says back room instead of bedroom as if he is inviting her to view a painting and not asking to get lucky. She has already gone this far, but there is a certain point beyond which she will not go. By this far, she means coming to his place. She has no intention of sleeping with him, however, and to enter his bedroom would make him think otherwise. As though the events of the early evening were not meant to lead up to this, she turns to face him and says, "I would prefer not to."

It sounds more prim than she would like, a guest declining the last deviled egg on a bed of lettuce.

He stops rubbing.

"This is too much like high school," Mikhail says without rancor, meaning she is too much like high school. Implying he's been mistaken in her. She isn't, after all, astute enough, modern enough, progressive enough, mature enough.

She is silent. Stiffly, she scoots away from him until her back touches the wall.

On hands and knees he crawls across the carpet to her. "Look," he says. "I'm sorry. I didn't mean it like that."

"It's okay," she mumbles, unwilling to let him know he's hurt her. She smiles weakly to let him see she is not accusing. She is unsurprised when he kisses her; she thinks it's his way of apologizing.

Her clothing does not come off, but articles of clothing are unbuttoned, unzipped, and unfastened. She is askew beneath him on the carpet, covered by his body, pinned by his weight and entangled by his limbs. There is no more kissing, no more rubbing. She is splayed like one of the books on his shelves, handled none too gently. She thinks he mistakes her shaking her head, her resistance, her pushing against him for something else though what the something else could be she doesn't know.

Afterwards.

"May I use your bathroom?"

Without opening his eyes, Mikhail points down the hall.

In Mikhail's bathroom, there is only one washcloth and bath towel on the rack. No hand towels for guests. Jamie rinses his bar of soap under hot water, then washes her face with her hands. She dries her hands on his towel, seeing the black smudge on her hand, a leftover from the party. They'd marked an X on her hand in magic marker so she could reenter the student center at will. At orientation, they warn you about what can happen at a party, what can happen on a date. But she was no longer at the party and she and Mikhail weren't actually on a date. Technically, tonight counts as nothing. Tonight does not exist.

She feels too tired to go back out to Mikhail's living room. Too tired to see him. Too tired to think. She goes further down the hallway to his bedroom, where she had not wanted to go before, and curls up on top of his covers. It no longer matters if she is back here.

Sometime later he wakes her up and says, "Think I should take you home now."

Jamie rises silently, wordlessly reaching for the thin jacket he's holding for her. Without his help, she slips herself into it and follows him out.

Mikhail opens the car door for her. He asks if she is hungry, if she wants to grab a bite to eat at either Denny's or Jack in the Box, the only two near things open this time of night.

"No. I'm not hungry."

"Sure?" he asks, belatedly solicitous. "It's no trouble. They're both are on the way."

"I would prefer not to," she says, wanting only to go 'home'—which is how she thinks of her dorm on campus—to her own bed, her own washcloth and her own bath towel, folding her hands in her lap and looking ahead on El Camino at the oncoming cars with their bright lights winking as if they know her.

We Wonder (Ode to Lisa Lisa)

Amina Gautier

...If we take you home, if our parents will kill us, or if they'll ever know; if our latchkeys are just the thing to help make this a go; if we should wait till they're asleep, or just do it when they're not at home, which is always. If they catch us it's all over. As soon as they get home from work they put us under lock and key. They don't want us to suffer what's happened to them—young lives over before they even have a chance to begin.

   ...Will you still be in love, baby? Or if you even are. You don't exactly say so when you call us over from your car and drive slowly to keep by our side, offering us rides, as we run the errands on which we've been sent. What we hear is "Yo, shorty!" "Excuse me, Miss," and jokes about jam versus jelly, all clues that one summer has made all the difference. We've traded in our short-sets for tank tops and Daisy Dukes, and we're women now—or at least on the brink, but we don't think anyone notices but you. At home we make ourselves useful. We pick up the dry cleaning. We babysit our younger siblings and make them afterschool snacks. We kill the mice. We take out the trash. We want so badly to matter and whenever we come outside your whistles and catcalls make us feel seen, so so flattered. Hanging out on the stoop with your boys, or leaning against your car, or just loitering by the pay phones, your eyes are on us, dogging our steps, watching us everywhere we go until it's so we can't escape the reach of those long gazes in a neighborhood that's only so big. All of this attention goes to our heads.

Because we need you tonight we'll wait till its way past dark to sneak out to the park and cut across the bleachers. We'll do our best to blend in among everyone who's old enough to be here, until you finally call us over. We let you lead us to your Mazda, your Jeep, your Escalade, your Range Rover. We let you adjust the passenger seat and tilt us all the way back till we're lying flat just like we're at home in our own beds. We take your advice and close our eyes—we don't worry our pretty little heads. "Just relax, baby girl," is what you say when your hand grips our thigh and you pretend to play with the fringe on our cutoffs. But the hand on our thigh climbs higher and higher— so high!— as your fingers dig and poke and pry. We fight the urge—we don't cry. You say *relax* as we squirm. You say *relax* though you can see it hurts. We wonder if it's too late for us to say "Stop," too late to say "Please don't." Will you still be in love, baby? No, of course you won't.

Former Virgin

Cris Mazza

When I heard this story a few weeks ago, I wished I could tell you about it. I don't know why. A guy named Roger told me the story about himself and someone named Wanda, but I didn't tell him about you. He might've asked why I don't see you anymore, and what could I have said, that I cried too much? I don't really know why. Do I?

If I *had* mentioned you to Roger, I would've had to tell him that you and I weren't the same as him and me. You knew me a different way. Didn't you? There's a way I could've explained it: Remember the time your wife gave me some of her old clothes? At first I was afraid to wear them, but when I finally came to work in one of the dresses, you said, "I recognize that dress," because no one else would know what you were talking about, so it was okay to say it. You smiled a funny way every time I wore one of them. I still have those dresses, and I still wear them, but no one recognizes them anymore.

Roger wouldn't've understood but it doesn't matter because I only saw him that one time. How would you look, I wonder, if I told you he and I were having this conversation in bed. But I won't try to imagine it. I wouldn't want you to know.

Maybe the only true similarity is that Roger was Wanda's teacher just like you were my boss. He was her graduate advisor. I don't know what he advised her in. He read her poems, analyzed her paintings, critiqued her plays, studied her clothing designs, discussed her photography technique, suggested good books and movies, played her songs on his piano? And he started calling her and visiting her in her windy one-room apartment where she served herb tea that tasted like dirt or perfume, and dried figs and hummus and pita bread. (Her bed was behind a curtain in the corner.) She had shaved her head a few months before and her hair was a soft one-inch long, making her tiny ears stick out a little. One of her dresses was a black parachute flak jacket. She also had a pair of tight black peg-leg jeans which she usually wore with a size-large V-neck man's undershirt. She put the V around in back. She wore her sweaters that way too. Once she showed Roger a pretty gray pull-over she said she'd bought when she was accepted into graduate school and knew she had to be more dressed up. Then she always wore it inside-out with the V neck in back and the label in front, under her chin.

"Too bad the label didn't say 100% virgin wool," I said to Roger, but I wouldn't want you to hear me say something like that, lying there naked in bed. You'll never know this about me.

But she was no virgin – it was too late for that. Not that it matters. Not that anyone is anymore.

Several times in the few weeks since I saw Roger, I've imagined telling you his story about Wanda, but I can't picture where we'd be. I couldn't have told you at work. You'd know why: In your office I told you things like my credit application was rejected and my car was dented while sitting innocently alone in a parking lot. I like to remember how you smiled and said, "Credit is easy, Cleo," and helped me make a new application. "Once you're credible, you'll wish you weren't." And you said the dent in my car would be a good reminder for me – that's what I deserve for allowing my car to remain innocent so long. But to tell you Roger's story, I would've had to shut the door, and it was a good policy, you said, that we never do that. Lunch was also not a good time for us to talk. Remember, I never said much at lunch? We used to go out with several other people and all sit together at a long booth where you would look at me from the corner of your eye, or across the table, and smile once or twice, or say something about someone else that only I would understand.

Of course there was that time I was at your house, but we had something else to talk about that day.

Most of Roger's story starts when Wanda came to his office after a seminar. She had left class early and he thought she'd come back to ask what had happened during the second hour and to find out when they were going to see the new Italian movie at the Guild. It was spring and had rained that day, so she had her black rubber boots and oiled parasol, and a black leather jacket over her white undershirt. He said her hair looked soft, like the fur on a little brown laboratory mouse. But her eyes, he said – he could never remember how her eyes looked, even a minute after she walked out of a room.

She sat as usual in the chair beside his desk and pulled her notebook out of her leather book bag. There was nothing held in the rings of the notebook, but between the covers she kept a yellow legal pad. She folded the pages over when they were full of writing, until the first ones got weak and came loose, so she had to fold them in half and put them between pages of her books. She also dug around in her bag for a pen, then tested it on the yellow paper. Tested it over and over, making curly-cue lines down both sides and across the top and bottom. She began coloring in the loops and said, "That woman who sits at the end of the table is really hostile, don't you think so, Roger? I'm sure she thinks I'm a spoiled little rich girl."

"What makes you think so?" Roger said.

"She's always late to class and never says anything. Or she sighs or says *hmmmm* or *Oh!*"

"That's a revealing perception." At this point Roger smiled while telling the story, and he brushed some hair out of my eyes which made my stomach kink-up and burn like hunger.

"Yes," Wanda said. "Do you think everyone has the wrong idea about us? The man across from me doesn't think I have anything important to say. He thinks I'm just trying to discredit him to make myself look better."

"Oh really?"

"Don't you see the way he looks at me over the top of his glasses – without raising his head – and he stirs his coffee while I'm talking, or spills it. When I tried to clean it up for him once, he said, *forget it – go on with what you were trying to say.* Do you remember that?"

Roger asked, "Is there some problem, Wanda?"

She seemed a little surprised and sat back in her chair, looking at him. He didn't even remember if she wore glasses or not. He said she had a very dainty chin and wide cheekbones. Her eyes may've been brown or green, he said. He'd been trying to remember. But *I* don't have any problem remembering: on your balcony, it was dusk, and as the sun set your eyes changed from blue to violet.

"Well," Wanda said in her same unsuprised soft voice, "I've been feeling uncomfortably anxious in class to the point where I don't feel I can sit there any more. I'm a distraction and it makes me nervous."

"This is absolutely lucid, Wanda," he said.

"What do you mean?" She cocked her head, only slightly.

"Well, you can't stand the thought that everyone might be paying undue attention to you, so you stand and leave the room, which causes everyone to stare after you."

"I didn't mean to disrupt the class."

"But isn't that why you left?"

"Certainly not!" She stopped doodling on her paper.

"I'm not chastising you, Wanda," Roger said. "I'm trying to help."

"I don't want our relationship to be based on you helping me." She still held her pen with both hands in her lap, twisting and turning it between her fingers, unscrewing it, fiddling with the insides, then screwing it back together.

"Do I make you nervous in class, Wanda?"

Again she was speechless for a second, but her hands didn't stop. She looked down at what she was doing to her pen. "I think," she said, her voice even higher and softer, "I shouldn't have chosen to sit so close to you."

Then after a moment Roger got up and shut the door of his office. When he turned around again, Wanda was standing behind him, and they embraced.

He said he heard the rain outside. Otherwise the room was silent. He seemed to have a difficult time telling me this part. He thought for a long moment, and I heard my clock humming, and right then as we lay in bed, I almost told him what I was thinking about: That evening, when you stood and went to the balcony rail, I rubbed my eyes and wiped my nose on my sleeve. The heavy air was salty. I heard you say, "Maybe there won't be a fog tonight," and when I could see again, I stared at your glass of red wine balancing on the rail.

They went to her place. Did I forget to mention that Roger was married? It doesn't make any difference; he and his wife had separate bedrooms. He found out that under Wanda's black jeans she wore black silk underwear, but under her white T-shirt she wore a simple white cotton bra. Then I think he felt a little embarrassed, talking about their sex while lying in bed with me.

He stroked my back and down over my rump. I told him it was okay. It makes me glad I'll never see you again.

When they were finished, Roger wanted to talk and Wanda wanted to go out. "Let's do both," she said. She got out clean black underwear and a clean white bra, but put on the same black jeans and white undershirt, then the black jacket and black boots. She stood at the door with her green parasol, jingling her keys in one hand.

She picked the restaurant. He said it was called Earth's Own Garden, and a whole side of the menu was dedicated to herb healing. "Nothing real happens in a vegetarian restaurant," he said to her, and she laughed. Her laugh, he said, was like a music box.

After they ordered he told her about his only other experience with a vegetarian restaurant. Someone was leaving the faculty and they were having a farewell dinner for him. Since he was a vegetarian, they chose a vegetarian restaurant. They were all supposed to meet there, but Roger had an afternoon class which ran later than usual that day, so he decided it wouldn't be worth it to go to the dinner at all. He called the place and asked them to page the party from the university. "I'm sorry," the hostess answered. "This is a vegetarian restaurant – we don't page our customers."

Wanda ordered the smallest salad and sat eating the alfalfa sprouts with her fingers, one at a time. He smiled and said, "What color are your eyes?" She stared at him and he still didn't know.

"You don't seem changed by this," he said.

"Were you hoping I would be?"

"I know *I* am."

"No you're not." She stirred her salad, looking for more sprouts.

He tried smiling again. "Well, it was a first for me – first time on a couch."

She found a sprout and ate it in three bites.

"Next time let's use the bed, okay?" he said.

"I don't like people to see my bedroom."

Roger ordered coffee. "We have grain beverages and herb tea," the waitress said.

"Don't you have anything dangerously flavorful?" Roger joked with her. She had thin brown lips. Wanda wore red lipstick when she went out, but her lips were pretty and pale when, before this had happened to them, he used to drop in to see her, unexpected, on Saturdays.

"I know what," Wanda said brightly. "Let's go to the theater on B street. They have a French movie. We can talk without disturbing anyone because they'll be reading the subtitles."

"We could go back to your place."

She was already standing, putting on her leather jacket. She turned, her hands in her jacket pockets. He said she looked like a young lovely punk.

"The heat's not working in my building," she said. "Didn't you notice?"

I wasn't chilly on your balcony until the sun was gone and a wind jumped out of the ocean. I rubbed the bumps on my arms. You never shivered. Your hands were steady as you looked through the telescope mounted on the balcony rail.

The movie had already started. Wanda leaned toward Roger to see the screen between the two heads in front of her. "Wanda, we do have to talk," Roger said. She was holding her wallet in both hands in her lap as she always did in the movies. "I don't want you to misunderstand," he said.

"You mean about our affair?" she said.

"I don't like that word. It doesn't have to be like that – cheap, secret."

Then Roger looked a little embarrassed again and stopped talking, even bent over to give my shoulder a sad kiss.

"It's okay," I told him. "I know there's a difference between her and me."

"Thank you," he said, touching my face again.

Wanda sighed and said, "Wonderful." She was looking at the screen, a wet black-and-white view of Paris.

"Wanda." He put his hand on her arm and saw that her fingers tightened on her wallet. But she did turn to face him. "Something important is happening to us," he said.

"Do you really think so?" she said.

"I want to know what *you* think."

"I'm flattered ... aren't you?"

"I just told you it's more than that."

Then Wanda said, "Oh!" and turned to read some dialogue on the screen.

Why wouldn't you stop looking through that telescope? There were no stars. The sky a rose-colored gray. I still remember everything. You knew I would.

"What's happening?" Roger whispered.

"Nothing yet."

"I mean to us."

She didn't answer. Her red lips parted. Her eyes moved across the lines of dialogue.

"I'm going," Roger said out loud. "I hope that you'll meet me outside."

She did come out, and she was smiling at him. She put her wallet in the pocket of her leather jacket and took his arm. But he didn't start walking with her. "Look," he said. "We have to make some things clear."

You never said anything like that. Maybe there was some fog after all, moving inland. "Pull yourself together, Cleo." You finally turned around, but stayed at the rail. "I think you want to look at the world through a Vaseline-covered lens." No lights on the balcony, but I could see your mouth moving.

"It's already clear to me," Wanda said, and she pulled so hard on his arm that Roger had to start walking with her.

"Then tell me how you see us." He said it was the same way they discussed her stories and plays: he told her nothing was happening and she said it was. But this was backwards.

Then she stopped outside a newsstand. "I catch my bus on the next corner, Roger," she said. She gave him a swift kiss on the cheek. "I'll be all right. I have to pick up something here. Drive carefully, it may rain again."

"Wait a minute!" She had already started to go into the newsstand, but he pulled her back. "I know you, Wanda – you starved yourself on grass for supper and now you don't want me to know that you're going to go get yourself some candy bars to eat on the bus!"

"Roger!" she gasped.

After a moment of staring at each other, he said, "It's okay, Wanda," and he touched her face. I shivered. He wasn't touching me then. He was lying on his back talking to the ceiling. He said he didn't remember what she looked like as she listened. His words came out slowly, his voice low, hard to understand. "Wanda, dear," he said to her. "Maybe you can't face the world without your alfalfa sprouts ... it's okay. I'd just like to be closer to you than anyone else has been – to be allowed to see you eat, sleep, maybe even cry once in a while." He *wanted* to see her cry. What does it mean?

Did he stop mumbling or did I stop listening? We lay there a while, then he said, "And you can guess what happened next, otherwise I wouldn't be here with you – Oh, I'm sorry."

"It's okay."

After a while I said to Roger, "How about if, after nailing you, someone told you you're not the center of the universe to anyone but yourself," even though you looked at me and smiled, your words spoken so softly, and the background was a dying day. You may remember what I looked like, but it's not how I look anymore.

Roger didn't say anything else. I think he left soon after that. I stayed there in bed for a long time. But only virgins cry.

The Sacrament of Brett

Roberta Montgomery

July 2, 1982

Bless me, Father, for I have sinned. It's been like, uh, what...
four days, one week and maybe three months since my last
confession? Since then I've, like, taken the Lord's name in vain a
bunch. I've lost my temper. I mean, I really lose my temper a lot,
particularly with my mom. I hate it when she asks if I've been
drinking. Duh! Like, many times. Everyone at Georgetown Prep
drinks. Unless you're a loser. Or gay. Oops! Sorry, Father. I like
beer. I really like beer. Hey, Father, do you like beer? And other
booze, too. Like, last weekend at the beach house I got totally
hammered on Everclear and Gatorade. I ralphed all over the living
room rug and the hallway and the bathroom. Squi said he had to
pull my head out of the toilet, but I think he was exaggerating and
trying to gross me out. I do know I passed out because I woke up
in the bathtub covered in baby oil and wasn't sure how I got there.
I've like, a ton of pressure on me from school and booze helps me
unwind. I'd explode like a rocket otherwise. Sixteen hundred on
my SATs won't get me into Yale? That's bullshit. Sorry for the
language, Father.

Let's see? What else? Oh yeah, I've disrespected my parents.
Like I said, they don't know how much I like beer. I lied to them
about what went on last weekend at the beach house. I said I was

going away to find peace and quiet so I could study. I took all my test prep books and my calculator and vocab flash cards and made a big show of putting them in the car. I said Timmy and Judge and Squi and me were going to do test prep together. The only testing we did was seeing who could drink the most. We joked around a lot, about boofing and devil's triangles and how easy Renate Schroeder is. Me and the rest of the guys are Renate alums. Heh-heh. But I am still a virgin, Father.

—*That's good my son. Chastity is the cornerstone of holiness and happiness.*

Well, I should be really happy then. For all these sins, especially the sins against Purity, Honesty, and Humility, I ask absolution and penance from you, Father.

August 3, 1982

Bless me, Father, for I have sinned.

It's been, like, two days, three weeks since my last confession? Father, I think about girls a lot. If you know what I mean. I guess you could say I have impure thoughts. I think about them all the time like a crazy hunger I can't feed.

—*That is natural, my son.*

But girls want nothing to do with me, Father. Especially the popular girls. I don't hate them, but they don't make it easy for me to like them either. At least that's the way it seems. Other guys know how to get somewhere with girls. I know guys who are crappy athletes and total stoners and losers who get tons of girls. I'm on the varsity football team! The captain of the basketball team! Still I get nowhere with girls. Who am I, the Hunchback of Notre Dame? I hit on a shy girl from Holton Arms. Two years younger. Not my type. Judge was in the room watching me go for it. He totally egged me on. She yelled for me to stop and bit my hand. Afterwards I jacked it. I mean abused myself, Father. I have abused myself many times. I got wasted that night and blew off Calc BC the next morning. I am letting my parents down.

I am sorry. For these sins and all the sins of my past life, especially the sins against Purity, Honesty, and Humility, I ask absolution and penance from you, Father.

February 20, 1984

Bless me, Father, for I have sinned. It's been two months and one year since my last confession. I took my roommate's parka without asking. And when he's out of the room I grab coins from his desk. I have been impure with myself many times. I have looked at pornographic magazines and once hid myself in the dorm bathroom to watch a girl shower. I masturbated. Twice I didn't return phone calls from my mother. I lied to her about the amount of money I need for books and bought alcohol instead. I have been drunk on many occasions. I like beer. I really like beer. Do you like beer, Father? I cheated on a test in Econ. I have disrespected women. At a party I shoved my penis in a girl's face. We were all drunk. Everyone laughed. It's not like I was hard or anything. The girl's name is Debbie and she's Puerto Rican. I bet that's how she got into Yale. I have been guilty of homosexual activity because when I hear my roommate masturbate it excites me so I masturbate. I made fun of a food server in the dining hall who is black and wears a hearing aid. I called him Little Deaf Sambo. All my friends laughed and now we all call him that. Probably I should stop. I wrestle with feelings of pride. I work hard. I'm smarter than most everyone I meet, even at Yale. I have a temper. I use the Lord's name in vain when I lose my temper. I ask absolution and penance from you, Father.

December 22, 1998

Bless me, Father, for I have sinned. It's been three months and two years since my last confession. These are my sins. I have missed Mass many times. I have committed blasphemy. When I lose my temper I take the Lord's name in vain. On several occasions I have drunk to excess. Beer mostly. I like beer. I really like beer. I have a temper. And I have intense feelings of envy... Our president? B.C., or Before Christ, as we call him in the office. A Rhodes Scholar? He hauls out his stupid saxophone to play "Heartbreak Hotel" on Arsenio and women swoon. Give me a break. We're going to see him impeached. . He'll be the second president in history. Let's see how smart he seems then.

—*Envy is a dangerous emotion, my son. Look to Mark 15:10, "For Pilate knew the chief priests handed Jesus over because of envy."*

B.C. is no Jesus, Father. He's an Arkansas hustler. He didn't inhale? *Right.* His IQ rivals Thomas Jefferson? *Right.* We're going to humiliate and destroy him.

—*The Capital Sin of envy can destroy you if not resisted. You must reject it and conquer these feelings through the grace of God.*

Father, can I still feel envy and be on the side of right? B.C. disgraced his office, the legal system, and the American people. He's going down.

—*When tempted to fall into envy, turn to Mary and pray to her, my son.*

Say a quick Hail Mary when tempted to be jealous. Be thankful and praise God with Mary's hymn of praise: "My soul magnifies the Lord and my spirit rejoices in God my Savior."

Father, I told Ken he should reveal every depraved detail we uncover. I'm adamant the people should know the truth and the truth is pure smut. The guy's a freak. You know he stuck a cigar in Monica Lewinsky's vagina? He had phone sex with her 15 times.

She sucked him off in the Oval Office. Nine times! He came in her mouth. Twice! In the Oval Office, Father! He beat off in a trashcan. He fingered her on the Resolute Desk. This is what's going on in the Clinton presidency? The People need to know. B.C. will be questioned under oath and forced to answer. He'll be disgraced. Father, I'm exercising my faith the best way I can, using the opportunities the Lord gives me, through the prosecution of righteous justice. I hate him, Father.

—*Hatred is not a sin, but St. Augustine advised, "Cum dilectione hominum et odio vitiorum," Hate the sin but not the sinner.*

That is a Christian goal that may be beyond me, Father. For these sins and all the sins of my past life, especially the sins against Purity, Honesty, Charity, Humility, I ask absolution and penance from you, Father.

October 11, 2018

Forgive me, Father, for I have sinned. It's been seven months and two years since my last confession. In the privacy of my home, I took my wife and daughters into my arms and lied to them. The fear in their eyes was assuaged as I passionately denied I ever touched that Blasey woman. My family's love for me is now pinned to that lie. And on the most public of stages I lied under oath to the nation. Yes, I fondled Christine Blasey. I locked the door and pushed her down on the bed and ground myself into her and ran my hands over her body. And when she screamed I held my hand over her mouth so no one would hear. That is her story and I believe her. Honestly, I was too drunk at the time to recall the details and offer a different, more convincing version of that night. What I do remember is it meant nothing to me. And I committed no sin of fornication. I deserve my rightful place on the Supreme Court. I am a righteous man. And I know the righteous way. Did you know, Father, that for the past fifteen years I've had the most conservative voting record on the D.C. Court? On the court I am serving God, damn it!

My face is everywhere you look, magazines, newspapers, television. My high school yearbook picture is seared into the nation's imagination. And when half the country sees my 17-year-old hopeful face, they see a sexual predator. When I was a teenager I got carried away. Groped a girl I hardly remember. The Clinton vengeance seekers and the #MeToo witches want to see me emasculated. If Christine Blasey Ford was their hero-victim I had to make myself into a bigger victim. That's what our President wanted. He wanted yelling and full denial. So I yelled and sniveled and cried, with my family forced to watch my humiliation. I lied. I perjured myself in front of the nation. Before you and God, I confess and tell the truth and ask for forgiveness. I represented myself as an innocent man because I was. I had confessed my sins! Isn't that the deal, Father? I got washed clean. Do you think the conspiracy wanting to deny me my place on the bench understands the sacrament? All they understand is vengeance, not the Lord's mercy. I will perjure myself in the court of Man. But until the honor of the Senate and the honor of God become one I will be judged by God alone. In the divine sacrament of our Lord I have been absolved. I have been washed clean. Believe me, Father, some day they will come for you. Do you know Matthew 5:10 father? I'm sure you do. It's become a favorite passage of mine of late. "Blessed are they who are persecuted for the sake of righteousness, for theirs is the kingdom of heaven." For these sins and all the sins of my past life, especially the sins against Purity, Chastity, Honesty, Charity, Humility, I ask one more time for absolution and penance from you, Father.

February 11, 2022

Hey, Father. It's been a while. Two years and three months since my last confession. Funny to be here asking you for forgiveness. I can't recall many sins. I guess the big one would be pride. Things are going very well for me. After being vilified by half the country as a drunken frat boy rapist I have won. And the church has won. Do we need more guns? More babies? Is it time to end Roe v. Wade? I decide. "Blessed are those who hunger and thirst for righteousness, for they will be satisfied." I am being satisfied, Father.

You know there are seven of us on the court, Father? *Catholics*, I'm talking. Seven Catholics out of nine judges. Is that wild or what? That's like one judge for every deadly sin. I chuckle when I think of that. I suppose this is where I ask absolution, Father. For all my sins. Especially the sins against Purity, Chastity, Honesty, Charity, Humility. That should cover it.

Superman

Victoria Patterson

My mother was raped when she was thirteen. She told me this when I was ten. She was drunk. She'd never told anyone before. "Men hurt women," she said. "But you'll be different." I felt like I already knew. She cried for no reason and couldn't stay sober. She didn't give details, and for a long time I created scenarios. I imagined her being pulled from the street by a ski mask-wearing stranger, raped behind the bushes or in a van with tinted windows—a knife at her throat—her dress ripped. Her screams muffled by a hand fisted in her mouth. I saw her collecting her clothes afterward, walking home in a daze. Not telling anyone, the shame. It was why she became an alcoholic. "When I got pregnant with you, Supe," she'd say, "I was a fifteen-year-old runaway, and it saved my life. You're my hero. That's why I started calling you Supe–like Superman." Her dad and younger brother were useless (her mom died when she was four), and I'd fantasize that I'd somehow time-traveled to protect her, living up to my nickname. I ascribed every bad thing that happened to her rape, and I carried it around like a backpack.

When I got older, and by older, I mean twelve, I learned that more often than not, the rapist is a husband, boyfriend, neighbor, or friend. Rarely a stranger. I asked my mom, and she said, "Oh Supe, I can't go there." I could tell by her face that it had been someone she trusted, and I began to wonder if it was someone I trusted too, a family member or friend. I wanted a name and revenge—but she said, "What's past is past, Supe." I began to wonder if the rapist was my grandpa or uncle or one of their friends. She wouldn't talk about it. "I should've never told you," she said.

For my thirteenth birthday, Grandpa and Uncle Billy took me paintballing on a patch of desert near Grandpa's house called Jackrabbit Pass. Mom stayed at Grandpa's house. She said she wasn't feeling it. Billy rented the equipment for offsite use, and he pulled it from his truck bed. I'd worn shorts–the paintballing was a birthday surprise, but Mom forgot to make sure I had on jeans. The paintball masks had goggle-like lenses that made us look like flies. I hurried along in step with my grandpa and uncle, through an opening cut into a wire fence and into Jackrabbit Pass—all I could see for miles was sand, sparse shrubbery, cactuses, and the mountains in the distance.

"Killing range," Billy said, his voice muffled from the mask, "is ten feet or more. Don't"—he shook his finger at us—"shoot closer or it'll fucking hurt."

"How're we supposed to hide?" asked Grandpa, his hand gesturing at the sprawling landscape. He flipped his mask up, so it looked like a hat, and then he lit a cigarette. He said, "Let's just kill each other and get this over with. Then we can go home and eat." He stared at me and flicked his ash. He paused, staring at me some more. "What's wrong with you?" he asked.

I flipped my mask to hat-position. "Something bad happened to Mom when she was just a girl," I said, meeting his stare.

Grandpa looked stunned.

"Say hello," said Billy, who hadn't heard us—taking on Al Pacino's *Scarface* voice inside his mask—"to my little friend." He backed up from us, aimed, and then hit Grandpa square in his chest. Then he fired at me—I moved—and he missed. I aimed back and nicked him on the shoulder.

We ran around and fired at each other for some time. It was fun. We laughed and yelled. Billy did clumsy faux-stealth somersaults. Then he got me in the thigh, and he wasn't ten feet away. It hurt and I fought tears, bending forward and sucking in air, the sand at my feet spinning. I flung my mask off to the side.

"You gonna puke?" asked Billy.

From my crouch position, I saw that they'd removed their masks and were staring at me. Grandpa has a flat, jowly-owl-face—whiskery eyebrows, hollowed out eyes. Uncle Billy has white-blonde hair like my mom's that looks alive and sticks out like a dandelion and long darker sideburns that go down his jawline.

"I have a mind," Grandpa said, "to shoot myself." He aimed the gun at his own leg.

I got to my feet and we all watched the bruise bloom on my thigh. My eyes were tearing. I pressed my palms against my eyelids. In the darkness, I said, "Mom was raped." I paused, releasing my hands. "She was my age." I looked at Grandpa—I don't know how to describe what I saw, except to say that his face looked empty, like you could fall into it and never land.

Billy and I exchanged frightened stares.

"You okay, Pop?" Billy asked.

Grandpa nodded, though he seemed to not comprehend what was happening. After a few minutes, Grandpa got his composure, and he and Billy asked questions. I told them Mom wouldn't tell me any more about it, and that I only knew that it happened.

Grandpa said, "It explains a lot," meaning, I suppose, why Mom ran away from home and became wild.

We agreed not to bring it up with Mom—she'd be mad if she found out I'd told them. I was relieved to not be the only one who knew and certain that Billy and Grandpa weren't Mom's rapist.

Before we left, Grandpa made Billy strip to his boxers, insisting I shoot him on his bare thigh in the same place. "Do it," he said.

"I can't," I said.

Grandpa—four, five feet away—raised his gun and fired a paintball at Billy's thigh. Billy yelled and bent over, his face pained.

Grandpa turned and headed for the fence. Billy, zipping his pants and buckling his belt, trotted after him, and I followed.

The rest of the afternoon had a hallucinatory quality, like time had slowed. Mom was stirring a pot of refried beans when we got back. She was drunk, doing her best to cover. I could tell by how she spoke—not the content, normal enough—but in the carefree rhythm, and how the words sometimes blended. "Supey-showertime," she said, as I was on my way to the bathroom to wash off the paint. She'd loosened up. Also Billy and I had come up with a lame excuse for the bruise on my thigh (I'd fallen on a rock), which she hadn't questioned. She could be a sleepy drunk. Her last DUI, she'd fallen asleep in the McDonald's drive thru. Her drowsiness felt contagious now—but not in a bad way—I just felt mellowed out and relieved too. We'd already agreed that I'd drive us home. I'd been driving since I was twelve.

At dinner, Grandpa poured beer into a glass for himself, and Billy drank from a bottle. Mom and I had ice water. She'd made Mexican food, my favorite. We filled our plates, passing around the beans, rice, tortillas, and then Mom said, "To Supe," raising her water glass.

"To Supe!" echoed Grandpa and Billy.

After birthday cake and presents (cash) everyone sat in front of the TV and then Billy turned on one of those Ironman Triathlons. A man staggered out of the ocean like a giant crab, dazed, while people cheered him on. Mom had a glass of pink fruit punch, which she'd spiked with vodka. None of us called her on it. She'd set a bowl of black olives on the table, because I like them.

"That man," Billy said, watching the screen, "needs to sit and rest."

Mom said, "When's the paintball portion?"

"Right after the archery," said Billy.

"You swim," Grandpa said from his easy chair, lifting his glass of beer, "ride a bike, and run."

Grandpa got up to use the bathroom and Mom sat in his easy chair, reclining it all the way back. "Pop warmed it for me," she said, drunker now, less capable of hiding it. "As a kid, I used to love sitting in his chair. It made me feel special and safe." She looked up at the ceiling and said, "I'm gonna close my eyes for a second." She went out quickly, snoring softly.

Grandpa came back from the bathroom and sat on the couch with Billy and me, his forearms on his knees and his hands folded. "I did the math," he said, "from when she was thirteen."

"Meaning?" said Billy.

"Rod Martin," said Grandpa.

Billy said, "Rod Martin? Your former business partner?" He looked at Mom sleeping in the easy chair.

"Following her around the house," Grandpa said, "like she was catnip."

My heart pounded.

Billy said, "Where's he live?"

Grandpa said, "Old folks' place in town; heard he went after Charlene passed."

Billy put a blanket on Mom. We left a note in case she woke, letting her know we'd be right back. Billy drove Grandpa and me in his truck, rumbling over the dirt road, smoothing out onto the streets and then the freeway. I sat in the middle. Grandpa stared out the passenger window. The mountains looked closer in the evening light, as if you could climb to the top. The fat moon rested on one.

Garden Nook Convalescent smelled like meatloaf, antiseptic, and medicine, and everything looked gray-green in the dim light. We asked a nurse where to go, and she said Rod Martin had dementia and it wasn't visiting time. She told us to leave him be. "Poor guy," she said. "Doesn't know his own name."

Billy said we wouldn't stay long, and that we'd just say hello, and then the nurse said, "Two minutes."

In Rod's room, another person I never saw was partitioned behind a curtain watching Fox news. Rod slept, skinny, shriveled, his mouth open. A surge of anger went through me, and I heard Grandpa say, "Wake him, Billy."

But I said, "No, me," and I stepped forward and grabbed Rod by the shoulders, digging my fingers into him, tightening my grip, his bones rolling beneath my thumbs and fingers. My teeth chattered. I shoved him back and forth like a rag doll, his head flopping. I pulled in closer, smelling his mothball smell, and shoved him down into the mattress.

His eyelids opened and his light blue empty eyes stared up at me. He tried to rise, flailing his arm, reaching out his hand. "Easy now," Billy said.

I backed away, trembling. Grandpa's hand went to my shoulder. "That's right," he said.

We stared at Rod, who had a goofy look—almost like a smile. He made a gurgle-noise and saliva pooled in his mouth, dribbling down a crease in his chin.

"This is useless," Grandpa said.

When we got back to Grandpa's house, Mom was still asleep in the recliner. The blanket had scrunched to her side. I covered her legs with the blanket and touched her shoulder. Mom sat up and looked around, scratching the back of her head. Her hair looked electric and she tried smoothing it with both hands. "Hello," she said, "this is embarrassing." She got up and shook out the blanket. Her cell phone fell out. She picked it up and sat on the couch.

"Do you remember," Billy asked, "Rod Martin?"

She shook her head. But she's a really good liar.

"Think about it," said Grandpa.

Mom's expression turned steely and she said, "I don't know anybody."

Grandpa said, "Okay, honey," and he patted for his cigarettes in his shirt pocket.

We said goodbye and Mom handed me the car keys. My grandpa and uncle followed us outside. They stood and watched while I adjusted the car mirrors. Mom rolled down her window, waved, and called out, "Go back inside. We're fine!" but they stayed and watched. Before we turned out of view, I looked in the rearview mirror and they were still there.

When we got back to the apartment, Mom said, "Let's watch Netflix, Supe." She left the bathroom door open and I saw her removing her makeup with a cotton pad.

We lay on the couch on opposite sides with pillows, our feet meeting in the middle. "You shouldn't have told them," she said.

I asked for more details: Was it Rod? Why hadn't she gone to the cops? Did she see him after? But she wouldn't say.

"Aren't you mad?" I asked. "Don't you want revenge? Your whole life could've been different."

"How?" she asked.

I wanted to say: You wouldn't hurt yourself. You wouldn't be drunk right now. But she knew without my speaking.

She looked at me sadly, as if she pitied me. "If my life had been different," she said, "I wouldn't have you."

Leaning back into the couch, she shifted and turned her head on the pillow. Then she was out again, and I watched TV alone, her toes touching my ankles.

Comeback

Jenny Shank

I kneeled down before the sandy-haired middle-aged-man who'd scarcely glanced from his phone to my face during our entire interaction and helped him ease his feet into the $300 Nike Vaporflys with energy-efficient foam that the Kenyans had worn to run a sub-two-hour marathon. World Athletics banned the shoes from competition, but big-spending hobby joggers still bought them for the alleged four-percent time reduction. This one's socks smelled like wet dog.

"How is that fit for you, sir?" I asked. It was a Saturday afternoon in September and SwiftSoles in north Boulder was packed. I hoped to earn enough in commissions to take some extra time off to train for the invitational in Oregon. That meant hustling each customer through their purchase to get to the next one without letting them perceive I was rushing.

"Sir's my dad," he said, running his fingers through thick hair he was clearly proud he still possessed. "I'm Glenn."

"Sure," I said. Glenn must be one of those guys who liked it when you took your time. "Glenn, how do these Vaporflys feel?" I never called them shoes. Everyone who bought them was seeking something beyond mere footwear. They wanted the triumphant experience of bounding, of running on trampolines. They wanted to know what it felt like to be a winner.

He examined my shirt for the nametag I never wore. "Didn't you used to be Jane Fontaine?"

I looked back at the wall with the picture of me winning the citizen's race in the Bolder Boulder 10k when I was 16. SwiftSoles was known for hiring pro and semi-pro runners and ex-runners as salespeople—it gave the store cachet among the amateur marathoners the town was thronged with. In exchange, the owners promised us time off for training and competitions. If you had once been famous enough, they printed a black-and-white photo of one of your wins and hung it on the wall. When my manager showed me the picture he'd printed without asking my permission two months after he'd hired me, I told him he could hang it as long as I didn't have to wear a nametag. In the photo I was freckle-faced and skinny-legged, my bones still factory originals, my hair in two long braids, joyful. I didn't look much like her anymore—my hair a shade darker and cut to chin length, my body fifteen pounds heavier, bags under my eyes. That girl had never worked for a living—she only ran. That girl scarcely ever lost, which was the opposite of the record I held now. But sometimes I thought if I stared at her hard enough, I could make her come back.

"No," I told Glenn. "That's not me." I didn't think of it as lying. I thought of it as telling my own version of the truth. For years I never got to do that—I had to listen to Coach Vincente's interpretation of reality and repeat it back to him. Saying what I wanted to still felt like a stolen lollipop: illicit, sweet. Coach Vincente used to say, "Much of what we think of as hunger is really thirst." But now I knew no glass of water could satisfy some needs.

"Coulda sworn," Glenn said.

"Yeah," I said. "I get that all the time."

"I heard she worked here."

This man—trustfunder, hedgefunder, young tech retiree?—was not used to people suggesting he was wrong. "Really?" I said. "I'll have to get her autograph."

"Wouldn't be worth much anymore." He chuckled. He thought he was making a joke, thought I'd laugh with him.

I yanked the laces on his shoes tighter.

"Hey, easy," he said with practiced sharpness.

I loosened the laces and he flexed his toes within the thick-soled wonder sneakers.

"Do these come in any other colors?"

A guy like Glenn liked to know all his options; he liked to know he was getting the best one. A woman like me, though, had whittled her promise down to few remaining options besides working at a shoe store and training on the side, and she needed to make this sale. "Black, lime, or blue," I said.

That evening at the track, Coach Hilda stood next to me on the starting line and squinted through her reading glasses at the numbers on her stopwatch. Her name wasn't really Hilda, but she'd told me to call her that ever since she was my middle school track coach, and when I'd begun to post startling times, she'd braided her long gray hair in pigtails to match mine as a way to root for me at a meet. "Hey, it's Brawn Hilda," a running coach with a beaky nose had said to his friend as we walked past him to the registration table. My coach was strong-shouldered, as broad as a shot-putter, and with her hair plaited like that, the man was saying she looked like Brunhild in a Wagner opera—the fat lady who'd sing at the end.

She stopped walking and turned to look at him, her blue eyes gone icy.

He ducked his chin, sheepish. He didn't think she'd overhear.

"It's Coach Hilda," she said.

On the starting line, Coach Hilda readied her stopwatch and told me to go. Today I was warming up with three and a half miles, and then transitioning to speed intervals. I took off, finding my rhythm, always enjoying how my muscles loosened after I ran the initial lap. Coach Hilda was the first to realize how much faster I was than everyone else during my sixth grade PACER test. My parents wanted to sign me up for a training club. Coach Hilda told them to take it easy. "Not too much, too fast." She didn't even really want me to join the interscholastic middle school team. She was the only one who ever looked at my times and concluded that I was something to preserve, rather than squander. Once I ran that first middle school meet, though, the secret was out. The club coaches swarmed my parents.

In high school, I took state records down one by one. I beat adults in 10Ks. I set national high school records. I won the 3000 meter at the World Junior Championships. I was winning so much instead of going to college, I joined Vincente's pro team in Oregon to train for the next Olympics.

I pulled up next to Coach Hilda after my fourteenth lap. My body was thrumming, my sweat starting to flow. Now I had my 400 meter sprints to complete, twelve of them.

Hilda clicked various buttons on the fancy stopwatch I'd given her, so she'd be prepared to time my splits. "Ready?"

I nodded.

"Go."

I ran down the first stretch, letting my pace increase as my shoes kissed the spongy, brick-red track. The waning warmth of the day released the rubber smell of the surface. Vincente was a running master I'd heard people talking about long before I ever met him, with his long, skinny face like a greyhound and a goatee tended as precisely as the gardens of Versailles. Everyone said he created champions. I knew it wouldn't be easy. Pain is the currency of running. But I was too young to know the difference between the kind of pain that built you up and the kind that broke you down. After I joined Vincente's team, nothing went according to plan. Somewhere between the weekly weigh-ins in front of all my teammates, the meager meals the coaches allowed me to eat, the diuretics and birth control pills they urged on me to drop pounds, and the arbitrary number Vincente fixated on for my ideal running weight, 105—twelve pounds lighter than I was—my body started breaking down. My period stopped. My bones lost density. I got a stress fracture in my foot, then my shin, then my femur. I came in sixth at the nationals and Vincente said, "You lost because you've got the fattest butt on the starting line."

That was why Coach Hilda always stood next to me on the starting line when I trained. "No matter what," she said. "The fattest butt will be mine."

I pulled up next to her and continued on my second 400.

"Seventy-three," Hilda called out as I passed her.

When I was working with Vincente, nothing would stop me—not the fatigue, the fractures, the humiliation, the poor results. "Your pain isn't real," Vincente told me after workouts when I'd rub my throbbing shin. I repeated what he'd said to myself, tried to make it my own truth. "Keep running," Vincente urged when I told him I was in agony. "Get to know this 'agony.'" But then I developed a hip impingement. I'd ground down my bones until they were sharp enough to tear my labrum. My body kept breaking until I finally paused to listen to it. What it had been screaming for three years was *stop.*

I zoomed past Hilda on the starting line again. "How does it feel?" she asked. "Seventy-two," she added.

I gave her a thumbs up and kept on running.

I came home to Boulder for arthroscopic surgery on my hip. The people I'd graduated high school with were college seniors by then, and I had nothing—no medals, no sponsorships, no future. I moved back into my parents' basement. My mom helped me with my ice machine and cooked me the kinds of meals I'd always eaten—small portions of stir-fried vegetables. But then Hilda heard about my surgery and came to visit. She brought me a huge pan of cheesy, sausage-stuffed lasagna.

I called out to my mom between mouthfuls, "Do you have any garlic bread?"

She looked at me like I'd gone mad. I hadn't eaten bread since I was an elementary schooler packing peanut butter sandwiches into my lunchbox.

Hilda had been angry at me for not accepting a track scholarship to college. But she also kept tabs on me, following my races. She visited regularly during the six weeks I was on crutches, feeding me pasta and Thai food, and offered to take me to physical therapy appointments sometimes while my parents were at work. Vincente never called. Instead, he sent a letter terminating our contract. None of the other people on the team contacted me either. They remained in his thrall, jockeying for the tiny, precious space my departure left. Not even Jake checked up on me. Jake was a lithe miler with sun-bleached hair who'd once given me a Valentine present, a small golden box containing four chocolates. He made the mistake of handing it to me after practice and Vincente saw. Vincente intercepted it, selected one chocolate out of it—caramel-filled, my favorite—and then pitched the rest into the trash. "You don't need those," he'd said, and then bit down on the candy. Jake never gave me another present.

"What's next?" Hilda asked, when I was mobile again and starting to build up my running slowly.

"The Olympic qualifiers are in two years," I said. "I want you to coach me." I wanted to try to qualify for the Olympics because that was what I'd always said I'd do. I thought maybe if I rejoined the path of my old dream, I'd find my girl self running there, unburdened, and I could merge with her and leave this tattered, grown self behind.

Hilda laughed. "I'm a sixth-grade gym teacher. I can cite the rules of pickle ball. I can inflate three dodgeballs per minute. I don't know anything about training an elite athlete."

"That's good," I said. "Because I'm not an elite athlete anymore."

She sighed. "I'm pretty old. I've been thinking about retiring."

She was in her early sixties. But I knew she had plenty of energy left. "You'd be bored without the kids." I thought of her in the XL Wonder Woman costume she wore to school whenever the kids met their Fun Run donation goal. "I trust you."

I wheedled until she agreed to coach me in exchange for discount athletic shoes. She'd always been a sneaker head. Now she had a fresh pair of shoes for each day of the week. I pulled up next to her after my last 400. She wore green Pumas because it was Saturday, and a matching tracksuit because she said it made her feel like a coach.

"Seventy-four," she said. "Cool down."

I had been running long enough that I had a decent idea of how to train even without a coach, but Hilda took it seriously, subscribing to *Runner's World*, checking out old copies of the *International Journal of Sports Science and Coaching*.

"Hey," Hilda said before I took off on my three-mile cool down. "Are you sure you want to go to Oregon?"

Oregon was where it all happened, where Vincente had broken me. Hilda knew all of the people who'd witnessed my breakdown would be there too, and that I could fail in front of them again. "The invitational is there," I said. "Where else am I going to go?" And before we could launch into an intense, emotional discussion, I did what I always did to avoid those kind of talks—I ran away.

On Sunday I went for a distance run over moderately hilly terrain in the open space west of town. It was here where I always thought I could see my unbroken girl self just ahead of me on the trail, on meadow paths I'd run over as an adolescent, my legs growing strong, the mountains rising before me. I tried to convince Hilda to show up but she said she was sleeping in. "Text me when you're done."

I was bending to tighten my shoelaces before I began when I saw the cult. A group of a dozen lean, focused men and women between the ages of thirty and fifty pounded down the path ahead, taking soft, dainty steps—the gentle footfalls of people with hours to cover on joints made of crystal. Their feet jingled with bells meant to ward off bears. The women's braids and ponytails barely moved as they rolled over the terrain, dust puffs rising at their feet.

I'd heard about them for years. The running cult lived together in a rental house, led by a bald, bearded guru who told them how long to run, how little to rest, what to eat, and whom to sleep with. He made them quit their former jobs and instead become freelance housecleaners, so they could earn money around the guru's rigid training schedule. They trained for ultramarathons, including a regular 50-mile Sunday training run. They often won these extreme competitions, some said because of that low-impact way of running they'd developed, and the way they'd shaped their lives around the running instead of the other way around. I used to make fun of them with my teammates—*Ew, that guru guy is totally gross!*—but now I wondered how far off their habits were from any of ours who'd gotten addicted to running. What was it about this sport that bred obsessives? What was it about running that attracted maniacal leaders who craved the power and speed of each new talent? So many people—from Vincente to the cult guru to the shoe store guy—tried to draft off the achievements of people like me, tried to subjugate us, tried to convince us we were nothing without them.

I ran after the cult down the path and mimicked their strides, copying the roll of their hips as they minced down the trail. A year ago, when my hip had started feeling better and I was running smooth again, a glimmer of my old dream had blinded me and I called Vincente to ask if I could come back and train with him again, to become a champion again. He didn't commit and told me to keep rehabbing, but kept a record of the call. Later he pointed to it to try to prove that he hadn't done anything wrong. "Why would she try to come back if I mistreated her?" he told one reporter.

But my plea to be allowed to return wasn't proof that he hadn't abused me. It was proof of how thoroughly he had.

In three months, I would travel to Eugene and assume my position on the starting line of the 5000-meter qualifier. It would be the first time I'd compete in two years. The others' gossip would make it back to me. They wouldn't hush their whispers enough for me not to overhear. But I would be ready. Coach Hilda couldn't be with me on the starting line, but her voice would be in my head, saying, "Remember, if they're looking at your butt— that's a surefire sign they're behind you."

As the trail turned west, I faced the red rock of the hills. The cult disappeared behind me and my stride grew natural, like I could go on forever. I told myself I was done with men telling me how far and how fast to run. With a middle school gym teacher for a coach, maybe I had no chance to make it back, but I wanted to work in secret this time. When you told people you were trying to make a comeback, they assumed you were trying to match what you had done—or almost done—before. I thought of it more as my comeback from the dead. A dead woman running is astonishing enough, whether she wins the race or not.

My lungs worked like bellows, rhythmic in exhalation, as the dry autumn air rushed into my nose. I felt what migratory birds feel in the fall, a stirring in their bones that commands them to take flight. I bounded over those rocky paths like I was in the middle of a dream of veldt migration. My legs felt so strong, it was almost possible to believe they had never been broken at all.

Potpourri

Christine Sneed

It always started with eye contact. Lucy would focus on one man until he felt the heat of her gaze, and if he looked back at her with a certain serious glint, she knew it had begun. He would ask the bartender to send her a drink, or else he would glide over and introduce himself before he ordered her an overpriced martini or glass of wine. It was best if he was over forty and not too handsome. The younger, better-looking men didn't have to pay for it, unless this was specifically what they were trawling for.

It was also best if the man she set her sights on had come to the bar with a group. Solitary men were bigger risks. A few were there purposely to look for someone like her. If she scratched beneath their veneer of public politeness, a strong hint of suppressed anger or resentment greeted her; they had something to prove, although some of them did not want to be bothered at all because their intention that night was to obliterate their personalities with alcohol, and in these cases there was no time or energy for anything else.

She did not do threesomes. She had no pimp or protector. She had a regular job. Sex with strangers was something she did on the side when she needed money, or was lonely and restless, or, on occasion, both.

Her birthday was tomorrow, her thirty-fourth. It was just after nine o'clock and she was in the Swissotel bar on West

Wacker Drive, drinking a gin and tonic, pretending to look at her phone as she surveyed the room. She was tall and slender; her breasts were real, her legs smooth and muscular from frequent runs. She was a natural blonde with hazel brown eyes. If asked her age, she told the men she was 27. Most of them believed her; some claimed she looked younger. She'd started sleeping with men for money the year after college when she earned a barely subsistence-level salary in the philosophy department's administrative office at the same university where she accrued eighty thousand dollars in loans over the four years she was enrolled as an international studies major. Even with three roommates, her rent and loan payments were more than she could afford most months if she wanted to eat something other than beans and macaroni and rice and go out with her friends a few times a month. Her parents were divorced and both said they didn't have any extra money to give her. She was, no surprise to her, on her own—as she had been, more or less, since high school graduation.

One of her roommates taught her how to work the men in the bars and soon she was doing it too. "Think of it as a second job," her roommate said.

She had rules: no bondage, no rough play, no blindfolds. Most men only ordered off the regular menu anyway.

In her late twenties, she was married for a few years and had stopped meeting men who paid to use her body during that time. She was faithful throughout the marriage—the sex work really had only been for the money; it was not some self-loathing, psychological trick she was playing on herself—at least she didn't think it was. Her ex-husband was married to someone else now and had a baby. She had never wanted kids.

A few months before her sixteenth birthday, she had sex with a friend of her father's, a man she had been attracted to since she was fourteen. She was a virgin when it happened, boy crazy, witlessly impressed by the purported physical ecstasies and intimate negotiations of adults. Her father's friend was somewhere in his forties, married, and drunk. His name was Carl Bonner and two years earlier, he had lent her father money to start a café that subsequently failed. At the time she hadn't believed he'd behaved badly with her because she had wanted to kiss him, and when he finally did kiss her, she wanted to keep kissing him, but the idea of anything more filled her head with the fog of alarm and fear, but also, confusingly, desire.

She gave in to his drunken cajoling in spite of her fears. It was over in less than three minutes, and it had hurt too, which she'd known to expect but hadn't realized it would hurt as much as it did.

Afterward, he told her they'd made a mistake, and that it wasn't something he'd ever done before. He told her never to speak of it to anyone because he would deny it if she did. Within the year, he and his second wife and their newborn son moved to another state. She hadn't seen or spoken to him since. His two children from his first marriage were closer to her age, but they went to a private school two towns over, and she wasn't friends with them. For a while she made herself believe she felt flattered, even lucky, that Carl had chosen her—possibly it meant he had found her irresistible.

In college, she met other girls who had had similar experiences, and they decidedly did not feel flattered. They felt angry and shortchanged and pitied her for not realizing sooner that she had been used in the most personal way. It bothered them too that Lucy did not seem to understand that a woman had the right to defend herself against unwanted attention by any means possible because it was the only way to be taken seriously.

She didn't know if this was true, because weren't women who fought back often made to believe they'd asked for it? Weren't they told that if they didn't look and act the way they did...that if they really did mean no, what were they doing at that party, wearing that top, drinking all those beers with those guys who they knew were a little wild, in the first place?

Sometimes when she saw a man who reminded her of Carl, she stared at him until he smiled or else looked at her with growing bewilderment. If she ever were to see him again, she didn't know what she would want other than his acknowledgment that what had happened was his fault. She wondered if he would still be attracted to her if he knew her now, or if he was plagued by remorse or a chronic, misplaced anger. Though of course he lived in some distant elsewhere, the past having swallowed him, and she had no intention of summoning him to the present. The past and its ghosts were best left undisturbed. If you brought them back, you could not hope to control how long they stayed.

This evening she was in good spirits and perfect health. She was so pretty that men and women both looked at her with curiosity and desire and envy. She knew that few people were as interested in the lives of the plain and the homely. To be plain or ugly was barely to exist, especially if you were a woman.

The man on whom she had set her sights for the night was in his mid- to late fifties, his dark hair turning silver. His suit was expensive, Savile Row or a convincing imitation. They exchanged steady, serious looks for twenty minutes before he raised his eyebrows, nodded, and came over to her side of the bar.

"I know you," he murmured, settling onto the stool next to her. He wore a light, almost flowery cologne. His nails were manicured, his face cleanly shaven. He had a faint accent—Italian, she thought.

"You do?" she said. "I think I'd remember you if we'd met before now."

"We've met," he insisted. "You worked at the University of Chicago, yes? The philosophy department. You were the assistant there. Laura, right?"

So he did know her. She would have to leave and start over somewhere else, or go home, but she didn't want to do either. "Lucy," she said warily.

"Ah, yes. Lucy." He took her hand and kissed it. "Nico Peretti. I know Mitchell Howard—Dr. Howard. I used to meet him for lunch sometimes, but now he is in California." He paused. "Do you still work in that office?"

She shook her head. "No. Not for a while."

"Are you—" He paused, his hand hovering above her knee. "Are you waiting for someone?" She looked down at his hand until he withdrew it and reached for the glass of wine he'd brought with him from the other side of the bar. He was fidgety, a little tense. His eyes darted around the room before they came to rest on her again. He was out of his depth, she sensed, but was trying to bluff his way through it.

"I have a friend who works here," she lied.

"It is a very nice hotel."

She gave him a small, cool smile. "Why are you here?"

"I like to look at the people. I come here sometimes when my wife is out of town."

"Only to look?" she asked.

He laughed quietly. "Sometimes a little more." He kept his eyes on her, neither of them glancing away. It was a peculiar thrill to look at a man this way, to be looked at in return with the same unequivocal challenge. *Yes? Say yes.*

Yes.

He moved closer, his mouth at her ear. His breath was warm, almost hot. His cologne filled her nose, the body beneath his clothes so easy to manipulate, so greedy to be touched. She took a long, surreptitious breath. She did like him, she supposed. A little. Enough. "Should we—" he murmured. "I'm divorced now, just so that's clear."

"Should we what?" she said.

His face fell but he blinked it away. "Why were you looking at me like that when I was on the other side of the bar?"

"I like to look at people too." She reached for her bag, a small beaded purse that held her car key, a credit card, condoms, pepper spray.

He took her hand and squeezed it gently. "Can I come with you? Wherever you're going?"

She didn't take any of the men back to her apartment. They always went up to a hotel room and once it was over, she collected her money and left.

"Do you want to go to another bar?" he asked. "Should we take a walk? It's a very nice night."

Outside the air smelled of chocolate from the candy factory several blocks downriver. So many people were out for a Wednesday night, but it was early August and warm and there was a celebratory frisson in the air. The Cubs were in the midst of a winning season. The streets were filled with tourists, money in their pockets, each with appetites to surfeit. Some walked in pairs or small, animated groups, others alone, hurrying toward whatever or whoever tethered them to their lives.

"Come home with me," whispered Nico before they'd finished crossing the bridge that delivered them to the south end of the Magnificent Mile, his lips close to her ear again. "If you won't let me come with you."

"Where do you live?" she asked. She hadn't made up her mind about anything yet.

"Very close. McClurg Court. Please?" His smile was beseeching. "I have thought about you since those days when I used to visit Dr. Howard. I wanted to come see you after he left, but it would not have been proper. I was still married then, for one."

"You can call him Mitch," she said. "I didn't call him Dr. Howard, not after the first week I worked there." She didn't remember Nico coming into the office, but it was probably ten years since she had last seen him, and perhaps he'd looked different then — fatter, bearded, less well dressed.

"I used to tease him about you," he said. "He would get angry."

She looked at him. "Why did you tease him?"

"Why do you think?" he asked. His throat and cheeks appeared flushed under the street lamps. Behind them two men laughed, loud and drunk, one crying out, "You wish, bro!"

"What did you say to him?" she asked.

Nico shook his head. "I'll tell you another time. I want you to think well of me."

They walked in silence for a moment, their hands brushing once. She pulled hers closer to her side, touched the cool, hard beads of her little bag. "What are you thinking will happen if I go to your apartment with you?" she asked.

He gazed at her, his red mouth twitching with a small, teasing smile. "That is all up to you, Lucy."

She turned away, glancing down at the water as they passed over the Chicago River, the bridge trembling beneath their feet as a CTA bus rumbled past, several people standing in the aisle, holding the hand grips, faces turned toward the smeared windows.

"Tomorrow's my birthday," she said before she thought to stop herself.

"So you're a Leo," he said.

"You know astrology?" She couldn't tell if he was being condescending.

He expression was wry. "Only a little. My ex-wife is a Leo like you."

"I'm divorced too," she said.

"Ah." His hand brushed hers again. "Did you break his heart?"

"No. At least I don't think so. I didn't want kids. He decided he did, and we were growing apart and so—" She shook her head.

"It isn't easy to unmarry someone," said Nico. "Even when there are no big battles." He paused. "Tell me, would you like to come to my place tonight? It is a very nice place."

She looked at him for a long moment before she nodded. She was curious about him and a little bored. She was also a little lonely—nothing, not even a dog or a tiny bird in a cage, awaiting her at her apartment. Her few good friends in the city were all but unreachable, lost to parenting duties and compliant monogamy.

He took her hand and kissed it again. "Very good," he said. "Very good, Lucy."

The pale, tall buildings on both sides of the street were lit up with commerce and blank promise, people flowing in a steady stream in and out of the stores, the hotel lobbies, the restaurants, their eyes giving nothing away other than their possession by the present moment.

Nico took her arm and led her on, his large hand warm at her elbow. She wondered if she could ask him for money. She wasn't yet confident she could accurately predict how he would respond to such a request. She wasn't going to ask, she decided then. With a stranger she would have been frank: Cash upfront, all right? *All right.* Or, *Oh. No, no, I don't*—*I didn't realize*—to which she would say, Sorry. A simple misunderstanding. But most of the time they understood and it went from there until they were done.

As soon as they entered his apartment, which smelled of some kind of vegetable matter going rotten, he reached for her and pressed himself against her. He was already hard, and she knew instantly that she'd made a miscalculation, assumed relative innocence where there was only subterfuge and cunning.

"Nico," she said, pulling back. "I thought it was up to me to decide what we did tonight."

His gaze was almost sorrowful. "Are you saying you don't want this too?"

She shook her head and stepped away. The thought arrived that she should go back into the hall, walk straight to the elevator and flee. Later, reviewing the events in her mind, she knew she would definitely have fled if he hadn't claimed they'd met before that night.

"We don't have to do anything," he said. "Or maybe just a little, if you agree? I want to see you without your clothes. I have imagined you naked so many times."

"That's creepy," she blurted.

He looked surprised. "Why do you say that? Young women's bodies are the most beautiful things on earth."

He led her away from the door, down a short hall and past the kitchen where she spotted a large bowl of fruit—browning bananas, a cantaloupe, a pineapple with its jutting, spear-like leaves—on a countertop littered with mail and coffee cups and dirty water glasses. He said nothing about the fetid smell. He had to have noticed it too but wasn't willing to apologize for it.

They entered a living room where a large, bare window looked westward over the city sprawl. The room also contained a plush, camel colored sofa and two matching armchairs. There was no TV, no stereo. Only the chairs, the sofa, identical tall lamps in two opposite corners, and a large glass coffee table. Nico turned to her with an eager smile. "The view is breathtaking, no?"

She nodded. "It is."

"May I get you a glass of wine? Do you like zinfandel?"

"I do, but I'm OK," she said.

He was disappointed. "Not even a little? I'd like to have some and it would make me happy if you did too."

"All right," she said. "But only a little."

While he was in the kitchen, she stood at the window and looked out across the city, its spires and towers and rooftops filling her with melancholy—their remoteness was both attractive and terrible. She knew she had to stop going to bars and taking money from men. There had been almost fifty of them. That was enough, she told herself. She also knew she would give in to Nico if he kept insisting, but she would find something to take from him in return—she did not want to leave him unscathed.

When he appeared with the wine, the glass he gave her was more than half full. He clinked his glass with hers before they each took a drink. The wine was unpleasantly alcoholic—the bottle had likely been sitting out for some time. When he turned away, she surreptitiously spit most of the mouthful she'd taken back into the glass.

"Tell me what you and Mitch said about me," she said after they'd settled onto the sofa.

Nico looked at her steadily. "Are you sure?" He put a hand on her knee and glided it up her thigh.

She took his hand and moved it back to her knee. "Yes. Tell me."

"He said he'd had dreams about you. Sex dreams. He'd wake up with a mess in his sheets." He was grinning hard as he spoke.

She glanced over at the window, at the constellation of lights, at the rooftops and chimneys in the near distance. She'd liked Mitch. He was the kind of man she would have picked up if he were in the habit of hiring a woman, but she doubted that he was. He'd flustered so easily and blushed sometimes when he'd talked to her. But perhaps he was different when he traveled. It would have surprised her, however, to learn that he was different in a different city, although it wasn't beyond comprehension.

"When I told him once I wanted to bend you over your desk and fuck you, he got very angry with me." Nico paused and took another sip from his wine glass. "I said he was acting like you were his daughter. I told him I knew he wanted to fuck you too. His sex dreams told me as much."

She turned her gaze back to him. His face was flushed, his pupils dilated. "What did he say to that?" she asked, noncommittal. Heat rolled off of him, his body burning with pitiless energy. He was poised to strike. She either had to leave or submit; this time she doubted he would let her pull away. "Wet dreams," she said. "That's what they're called."

He laughed. "Call them whatever you want. You know what I meant." He leaned in to kiss her and she let him, fear and lust rising in her chest. When he pushed her skirt up to her waist and pulled down her underwear, thrusting his face between her legs, his tongue immediately finding the right place, she was stunned. The sofa's fabric was velvety against her bare arms, her nerves tingling from what he was doing to her with both skill and patience. He kept going, softly, inexorably insistent until she came, her cry making her ears ring.

She was still gasping, her vision not yet cleared, when he unzipped his pants and began working himself over with a hand he'd spit into with almost clinical precision. Within seconds he too was coming with an anguished groan, his head flung back, and then it was over, both of them wordless and panting, still mostly clothed.

She almost never had an orgasm with a man anymore. She wasn't sure if she wanted to offer him something else, but he was already standing up and stepping away from her, the air around him appearing for a second to turn darker, almost fog-like. She struggled to put on her underwear and smooth down her skirt, unable to think of anything to say. He disappeared into the kitchen where she could hear him take a glass out of the cupboard and run the tap. She pictured the fruit moldering in the bowl and lay back on the sofa, her body still throbbing. She hadn't come like that in a long time. He was unnerving and rude. She realized with a feeling of both confusion and resignation that she would see him again if he asked her to.

It seemed unlikely there would be a second time, however. At the door a few minutes later, he handed her a hundred dollar bill. "Is that enough?" he said. He looked more tired now than smug or cunning. He looked older and resigned, wearied by the series of choices that had led them both to this moment.

She stared at him, wondering how he had known. She almost didn't take the money, but there it was. He pressed the bill brusquely into her hand, impatient to have her gone, and she put it in her bag and heard herself saying, "Yes. Thanks."

He closed the door without a word. Her face was burning, heat creeping up from her neck. It took a second to remember which way the elevator was. No sounds emerged from behind the clean white doors of the other apartments she passed in the hall.

A bowl of red and brown potpourri, cinnamon scented, sat on a table in between the two elevators. She found herself touching the wood chips and cloves and bristly dried flowers as the elevator doors opened. Before she recognized what she was doing, she dumped the bowl's contents onto the floor.

On the ride down to the street and during her flight across the city in a taxi where neither she nor the young, goateed driver bothered to speak, the stink of Nico's apartment stayed on her. It wasn't until she was home and had taken a shower that she let herself fully breathe again.

How to Walk on Water

Rachel Swearingen

I'll show you the backside of your soul. That's what Arvel Wilkes told Nolan's mother, Sigrid, the night of the attack. Nolan had found a manila envelope with a smeared carbon copy of the original police report inside. Sigrid had been just twenty-six when it happened, younger than Nolan now. The report didn't note what his mother said in response to Wilkes, just that there were "minimal defensive marks on victim." They had been living on the north side of Seattle at the time, his father away on a business trip, Nolan asleep in his crib.

He was home to pull his life together, staying in his mother's guest room, trying to keep out of her way. She couldn't fall asleep without the radio. She left her bedroom door ajar for her cat, and Nolan crept closer to listen. *Was Princess Diana's death a setup? What about JFK Jr.? We're going to hear from a man who claims there is a secret profession of accident staging. Later in the hour, I'll be opening the call lines. Do you believe in evil? What led you, or someone you know, to a moment of evil?*

"Too loud?" Sigrid said. She must have sensed Nolan standing outside the door. "I can turn it off."

"I thought you called me," he said. She tuned in to the same station every night. Aliens. The supernatural. Government conspiracies. Time travel. It wasn't like his mother to listen to such things. "I'm going to bed now," he said. "I'll make sure the doors are locked."

He went into the guest room and shut the door. His mother's desk was there, her photo albums, her boxes of tax and financial records. He'd found the envelope, along with a recent letter from the Seattle Police Department, while rifling through the desk for her checkbook. Arvel Wilkes had died in prison. She hadn't mentioned it.

Nolan called his father in Pensacola and told him he'd been hunting for information, that he found a medical report and knew Sigrid could never have another child. "Is that why you divorced?" he asked. "Is that why she never dated anyone?"

His father still loved Sigrid. It hadn't been his idea to separate, and Nolan suspected he'd finally left and remarried because there was no going back to the way it had been. "You always liked to pick at scabs," his father said now. "Never could leave well enough alone."

"Dad, I'm worried about Mom. She's into all this UFO and shadow government shit. She's losing it."

"She never says nothing to me about UFOs. I talked to her the other day. She's worried about you. She said you just sit around on your ass all day. She thinks you're depressed."

"So you and Mom didn't split up because of what happened?"

Nolan could hear his father rattle ice in a glass, looking for the perfect cube to chomp. "Your mother and I are OK," he said, biting down. "We're just different people, that's all. She met someone she could talk to back then. She couldn't talk to me."

"Who?"

"That was a long time ago. Don't bring up Wilkes with her. You let that monster rot."

•••

"How did the job search go today?" Sigrid asked. She filled a watering can and fussed over a plant on the table where Nolan was paging through a newspaper. Somehow the day had gotten away from him, and he still hadn't showered or shaved.

"Nothing yet," Nolan said. "I'll find something."

Over the past few years, he had lived in towns all over Colorado and Wyoming, working as a bartender, a rental manager, a warehouse supervisor, and a short-order cook. He had borrowed money from Sigrid to build his own food truck, but that project never quite got off the ground. His most recent venture was with his ex-girlfriend, Brenda. That winter they'd paid for rent and ski passes with insurance payments for a bogus accident. When the money ran out, they called college kids about bank errors, trying to get their usernames and passwords to drain their accounts. They managed to get a hold of one unsuspecting girl's password, but when they logged in to her account, the girl had just ninety-two dollars. "Well," Brenda said, "At least we know how to do it now. That's a start." But for Nolan it was the end.

He was almost thirty and tired of dead-end jobs, of falling in and out of love. He waited for Brenda to go out and called his mother to ask if he could come home. It had been two and a half years since he'd seen her. To his relief, Sigrid hadn't asked many questions. She just said she'd had a feeling he would call, and then she wired him money for airfare.

She sat down now with a cup of hot water and a slice of lemon. "You should call some of your old friends from high school."

He glanced up from the paper and stared. They'd been through this all before.

"Well, there's got to be someone," she said. She was semi-retired and worked part-time for the city clerk, even volunteered at a literacy center downtown. She brought home university extension catalogs and left them on the table for him. "It wouldn't take much, Nolan," she'd say. "Just five or six more courses."

She was about to start in on him again. He had gone to college in Boulder on a diving scholarship but dropped out after a few years. He didn't want to hear it. On the refrigerator, she had a magnet that read *Talk is Cheap*. He couldn't mention Wilkes to her, but she could listen to harrowing stories on the radio all night long.

"Why do you listen to that show?" he said. "You don't believe that shit, do you?"

"What show?" She was taken off guard, and then she laughed. "Oh, you mean my radio program?" She twisted the lemon and dropped it into the cup. "It's quite entertaining, really. Better than those political ones. I can't stand those."

"And you don't get nightmares listening to alien stories?"

"See," she said. "You can't help listening either." She studied him. "It's funny having you here. I feel like I need to get to know you all over again." She stood and opened a cupboard and looked inside. "Do you still like the curly noodles? I bought some for you. Remember how you wouldn't eat spaghetti? I couldn't convince you it was made out of the same ingredients."

He folded the newspaper over, snapped it to let her know he was trying to read. He'd scanned the paper in five minutes that morning, and now he read the same article about a missing child that had been found in Oregon and brought back to his family in Minnesota.

"When you get an interview, you'll have to wear a button-down and cover those tattoos." She wanted to know if he regretted getting them now.

"No, Mother. I like them."

"Really? Even that cartoon one? Remember how you hid it from me?"

When he was eighteen he'd had the Tasmanian Devil inked on his forearm. He thought it would make him appear both tough and funny. It looked more like a bloated squirrel, not that he'd ever admit this to Sigrid. She worried about his pierced ears, too. "They look like bolts, Nolan. Like Frankenstein. That can't be sanitary. You'll stretch them out. Someday that won't be in style, and then what will you do?"

He stared at the thin scar jagging up her cheek and across her temple. It was barely perceptible now, and she didn't even bother trying to hide it. "I'm sure I'll be fine," he said. "It's just skin."

"Oh, I know," she said. "But you know how people can be."

•••

You know me, Wilkes had said to his victims, and he meant it literally. He'd worked at the neighborhood grocery store as a bagger. He'd held crying babies while mothers loaded their carts, chatted with husbands waiting outside in their cars. No one suspected him, not at first. Sure, his coworkers wondered why he didn't have a better job, why at forty-three he still lived with his mother. They all agreed there was something "off" about Wilkes, but he seemed friendly enough.

Sigrid had other scars too, on her legs, on her torso. When Nolan was growing up, she'd told him they were from an incident when he was a baby. He had always thought she'd gotten into a car accident, and not even his father had told him the real story until he was in high school. "Your mother didn't want to burden you, that's why," his father said when Nolan asked him why they had lied. "She white-knuckled it for years. For you, kid."

Nolan shut the door of his room and pretended to search for jobs on Sigrid's slow desktop computer. He pushed his suitcase up against the door and pulled out the report. Somewhere in a police department basement were the originals. He imagined his mother in a hospital bed, two detectives pressing her for details. His father had told him that much, that they played good cop, bad cop, that they made her tell her story over and over. His father had thrown a fit and almost landed in jail.

The detectives must have asked Sigrid to list everything Wilkes said and did. *You're not very pretty, but I will show you your soul. It is a sneaky thing. We will have to work very hard to get it all.* Nolan knew his mother. She'd lived in Seattle most of her adult life, but she was still a stoic Midwesterner at heart. She would have reported just a few of the things Wilkes said, leaving out the worst details. She couldn't stand anything lurid. She hated emotional displays.

That night she had left Nolan with a babysitter and gone to the Oasis tavern, where Wilkes was drinking. She'd told the police he must have followed her home, but there was some question of whether she might have accepted a ride, whether he had waited outside for the babysitter to leave. There was no sign of forced entry. Sigrid told the officers she might have forgotten to lock the door. They knew Wilkes's profile, knew his victim type: petite, new mother, what they later described as a "reluctant Madonna type." By then they had gathered a list of women who had disappeared from the area, but they had only circumstantial evidence linking them to Wilkes, and no bodies, yet.

• • •

When Sigrid was out during the day, Nolan watched TV and took long baths. He stole twenties from a soapbox his mother hid in her dresser and felt like a teenager again. He had no money, just what little she gave him for spending. In his suitcase, he had two blank checks from her desk. He just needed a few weeks to clear his head. If things worked out, he'd tear them up and she'd never know. If not, he'd cash them on the way out of town. He kept a six-pack of cheap beer in the refrigerator and replaced what he drank before Sigrid returned in the evening. One afternoon, he tried to recreate the aftermath of the attack by pulling himself out of the tub and crawling across the tile. He hadn't gotten very far. He only managed to scrape his knees and scare the cat.

When Sigrid came home, she said, "What's this water all over the floor? Did you spill something?" He told her he had taken a bath and forgotten his towel, and she had looked at him queerly and said, "There's a shower right next to your room."

In *The Seattle Times* online archives, Nolan found an article from when Wilkes was put away for Sigrid's assault and rape in '84. In the picture, his face was boyish, his blond hair thinning, and he had dull, close-set eyes. If Nolan had passed Wilkes on the sidewalk, he would have never given him a second glance. They had failed to get Wilkes on attempted murder. He was out on parole eight years later, lived just hours from Sigrid for twenty more years, until he was finally convicted of the murder and dismemberment of a young woman in Coeur d'Alene, Idaho. He'd confessed to killing six others, though investigators believed there were many more. Nolan was in Colorado when he heard the news and called his mother. She told him detectives had been visiting her for years, trying to put Wilkes away. She'd said this like it was just another piece of passing news.

•••

At the pool, Nolan changed into the new trunks Sigrid had bought him and took a shower. When he looked in the mirror, he didn't recognize the man staring back. He had a paunch. His chest was a little sunken, his tattoos faded from years in the sun. His shoulders were no longer the shoulders of a swimmer. He walked along the edge of the pool, past a children's swimming class to the lanes reserved for laps.

He didn't have goggles, and the chlorine stung his eyes, but he was surprised how quickly the strokes came back, how his arms and legs remembered, how his breath fell into a rhythm, how he simply turned into the next lap. He heard his coach's voice in his ear. "No resistance, Nolan. Don't think. Just swim." He couldn't get that lightness though. He felt himself straining, fighting the water, allowing his arms and legs to create a drag, to chop instead of slice. He hung onto the edge of the pool to catch his breath.

When Nolan was five he'd tried to walk on water. Sigrid had been trying out religions then. She took Nolan to a Catholic mass, and afterward Nolan joined the kids in the church basement, where they colored pictures of Peter walking on water toward Jesus. One of the sisters explained that a sudden wind had frightened Peter and he lost his faith and started to sink. She asked the children, "Do you believe?" and all the children nodded, and Nolan believed too.

He had gone to the beach at Golden Gardens with family friends a few weeks later. He led another boy down to the marina and walked to the end of a dock, sailboats moored all around. He said, "Watch," and then he stepped off the pier, thinking of Jesus, and he was genuinely shocked when his feet slipped through the surface and he was underwater, thrashing, his ears pounding, his lungs seizing. A man jumped in after him and lifted him onto the dock. He hadn't been there, and then he was. The next day, Sigrid signed Nolan up for swimming lessons, and the rest of that summer she forced him into the water over and over until he was too tired to cry.

The man in the next lane moved slowly, crashing forward, kicking up huge waves. A woman swam against his wake, and she stopped now and then to recover before starting again. The diving board gave Nolan a feeling of vertigo, but he couldn't stop looking up at it. He hadn't dived in years, not since training for the conference championship when he was a junior in college and botched his first dive, only to blow out an eardrum on the second. His ears healed, but he gave up. He didn't even formally quit. He just left school and never returned for his senior year. His father was furious, but Sigrid told him he could always come back home and finish school there. "There are worse things," she said.

The man in the other lane looked satisfied as he pulled himself out of the water and his feet slapped the wet tile, thrilled that he had finished however many laps he had set for himself that day. On the other side of the pool, toddlers were getting lessons, and Nolan thought of Sigrid jumping in with him for his own first lessons, though she couldn't swim herself. He still remembered her scars when he opened his eyes and tried to dive around her, how they wove up her legs, raised and thick as vines.

•••

Sometimes Nolan talked to Wilkes in his head. *Why'd you do it, you miserable fuck?* Sometimes Wilkes answered him in a nasally voice that sounded from a distance. *I'm upside down. Do you see me up here in the corner?* That's what he'd said to Sigrid when she was lying in the tub, passing in and out of consciousness. She told the detectives he'd talked like he owned the voice of God.

Nolan tried to imagine Wilkes's face, to slowly obliterate it, but he kept seeing his mother instead, in a yellow dress, her hair freshly washed and smelling like strawberry shampoo, walking into the Oasis, happy to be out of the house for the night, away from her baby. According to the police report, she had gone alone but hadn't noticed or talked to Wilkes, though other witnesses placed him there sitting a few stools down. Next to Sigrid's words, the detective had scribbled a question mark and circled it.

A witness claimed that Sigrid had talked to several men that night and that she was wearing a miniskirt. In the report, the word "miniskirt" was underlined twice, as were "two brandy old-fashioneds."

After Wilkes was through with Sigrid and left her unconscious in her bathtub, he went to the hardware store for a tarp and then stopped back at the tavern before heading back. The detectives thought this was to solidify his alibi, but Nolan pictured Wilkes sipping his cold beer, a barely detectable smugness on his unremarkable face. He might have gone to the tavern to celebrate, to draw the experience out. Meanwhile, Sigrid had come to and inched out of the bathroom and all the way out the door. A neighbor found her on the front lawn, unconscious, wearing nothing but a bloody towel. Nolan had slept through it all.

He folded the report and slipped it into the manila folder and closed the flap, wrapping the dry, brown string around the clasp.

He had moved a second radio into his room and turned it down low. People called in from all over the country. Truckers told tales of haunted rigs and ghost dogs in the road in the middle of the night, and he could hear the highway around their husked voices, see them sleeping in their cabs at rest stops. Others called about the feeling of *déjà vu* right before a calamitous event, or about seeing loved ones moments after they died.

He turned the radio down and heard the same muffled voices coming from his mother's room. The harder he listened the more he heard a split-second delay between them, and he lay awake trying to blend the sounds together again, trying not to hear an echo.

•••

They were having lunch at the kitchen table, eating cucumbers on rye with tomato soup, and Sigrid handed Nolan a napkin. It amazed him how little she ate. She looked like a grandmother now, her eyes smaller, nearly lost in lines. She wore long skirts and round-necked sweaters and flat European shoes. She had matured into her name, into her condo with its blue and white teacups.

She set her sandwich down on her plate. "I don't want you around here all day, brooding. It's making me crazy."

"Why? You're not even here most of the time."

He wanted a burger. She used too much butter. Thick slabs of butter. She had very little in her refrigerator, but she had plenty of butter. Nolan stood and tossed his uneaten sandwich into the garbage. He grabbed a beer and popped it open, watched Sigrid ignore its slow hiss.

"Life goes fast, Nolan. It's the things you don't do that you'll regret."

"Really?" he said. "I wonder what Arvel Wilkes would say about that. You let him in. Didn't you, Mom?"

She folded her napkin and dropped it on her plate. "You've been going through my things again. I want you to stay out of my papers. I don't know what you think you'll find."

"You probably offered him a sandwich. With butter. Lots of butter."

"You're just trying to upset me," she said. She stood and rinsed her plate and put it in the dishwasher. "Why are you being so ugly lately? Why did you come back here if you hate me so much? What is it you want?"

"Nothing, Mom."

"Well, obviously, it's not nothing." Her back was to him. She didn't turn around. She bent down to pull a bucket out from under the sink. "Get out of the kitchen. I'm going to scrub the floor."

"Mom," he said. "I'm sorry. Jesus. I'm sorry. OK?"

She filled the bucket in the sink. "I don't know what it is that makes you want to hurt me. I don't know what I did. But you have no right. Not about him. Not about that."

•••

Nolan nudged the radio closer. He gasped out loud when a caller mentioned seeing a purple disc of light above the mountains in Santa Fe. When a woman called to say she went hiking and returned to the parking lot to discover that she'd been gone for three days and could only remember a flash in the sky, a metal table and probing instruments, Nolan surprised himself by uttering a faint, shocked, "No way." In a way, he supposed, something similar had happened to him. A flash and years gone by, and he had nothing to show for it, not really, not even a pot to piss in, as his father would say.

Late the next morning, Sigrid opened the blinds by the bed and said, "I'm beginning to think your father was right. I'm doing you a real disservice letting you stay here."

"I'm getting up, Mom." He turned over and burrowed into the pillow.

Sigrid stood at the end of the bed. "Did you take my checks? I'm missing two checks and I want to know if you stole them, Nolan."

"What are you talking about?" he said. He sat up in the bed and looked her straight in the eyes. "I don't have your stupid checks. Maybe you forgot to write them down."

"You're going out today, and I'm going to lock the door. I don't care what you do, but you're not staying here. I want you to give me your key."

He sat up. "You've got to be kidding. I'm not a child, mother."

"Tell me about it," she said. "I'm calling the bank today, too."

•••

After he dressed and stuffed the blank checks into his pocket, he hopped a bus to Belltown to wait with the day laborers for work. Every city had a corner like this one. People would pull up in their trucks and SUVs with odd jobs, and men would clamor about, arguing over whose turn it was next. Nolan tried to get the jobs requiring two or more workers. He didn't like going to someone's house alone. Once, in Denver, he went with a man to his mansion in the suburbs to shovel truckloads of gravel onto a long driveway. The man told him he'd pay twenty an hour, but at the end of a full day he gave Nolan fifty bucks. Nolan had nearly pummeled the guy. He was left without a way home, but he took the fifty dollars and threw it on the ground and said, "You need this more than I do." It wasn't true. That night he went out to a bar and got into a fight with a guy more down on his luck than Nolan, and by the next morning he was facing a five-hundred-dollar fine and community service.

He'd been waiting for over an hour, standing back from the other men, feeling the draw of the clean paper checks in his back pocket. He'd find someplace to cash them and get out of town. Leave his suitcase at his mother's. She had plenty of money. She'd be fine. Then a young couple pulled up. It was just a few hours of work, helping them move. He hopped into the truck with a tiny Ecuadorian guy named Rolando, and they drove up to a house on Phinney Ridge and hauled furniture and supermarket boxes filled with books into a rental van. Rolando lifted two boxes for every one of Nolan's, and Nolan worked harder. Sweat poured down his back. Not everything would fit in the truck, and the couple started arguing. Finally the woman paid them and said they might as well go.

Sigrid had called and left a message on his cell phone, telling him she was going to grill steaks that night, but Nolan didn't want to go home. He felt itchy and wild, and he and Rolando walked downhill to a bar in Fremont filled with college kids and hipsters. The beers were six dollars a pint, too much for Rolando. "Come on, man," Nolan said. "Let me buy you one." Rolando looked around warily, and Nolan couldn't convince him to stay. Nolan drank one pint while pretending to watch a soccer game on TV. A hot girl in a sundress stood next to him, her arms inked in colorful, intricate designs, and he watched her until she turned around. "I like your tats," he said, and she looked frightened and slid deeper into the crowd. He needed a shower. His shirt was striped with sweat and dirt. He set his empty glass down on the bar and slipped outside to wait for the next bus home.

It was almost dark by the time he reached the condo, but Sigrid grilled his steak on the patio in her pajamas and robe. He could tell she felt bad about accusing him, about making him leave for the day. She placed a cold beer next to his plate and sat down to watch him eat. The work and the walking had given him an appetite, and he knew she was waiting for him to tell her how good the steak was, to tell her about his day.

"You were always so good-natured, Nolan. What happened? Why are you so angry? Did something happen to you?"

"I'm not angry, Mom. I'm fine."

Sigrid hugged herself against the chill. "It's not good to keep everything bottled up."

"You ought to know."

"You're just itching for a fight. Your father called. He's worried about you."

"Everybody's worried," Nolan said, but he was too tired to keep arguing. The last of the sun slipped behind the ridge, and they went inside, and Nolan washed the dishes while his mother got ready for bed.

In the envelope with the police report, Nolan had found a dried wildflower and a handwritten message on police notepaper. *We'll make it, Sig, if we stick together.* Maybe Sigrid had fallen for one of the cops that questioned her. Maybe this was the man his father meant, the one she talked to when she couldn't talk to him.

Maybe the good cop said, "You're lucky to be alive."

"Luck," the bad cop grunted. "You call that lucky?"

His mother would have preferred the bad cop. When she finally spoke the words Wilkes said to her, it would have been to him.

The bad cop didn't try to comfort. He let her see the crime scene photos, though it was against rules. He would never have said, "It wasn't your fault. You couldn't have fought back." He suspected they'd find others buried somewhere. "Life is shit," he would have said. "Luck is staying alive."

•••

Sigrid was asleep when Nolan left the house again. He could hear her radio as he snatched her car keys from the hook on the kitchen wall. He drove to Aurora Avenue, looking for the tavern where his mother had met Wilkes. The street was still lined with greasy diners and Chinese restaurants, seedy motels with vintage neon signs. *Free Local Calls. $55 a night. Vacancy.* The Oasis still existed, squeezed between a tire shop and the run-down Rosebud Inn with its painted sign bleached to pink and weeds sprouting from the lot where he parked.

Inside the tavern, dusty luau flowers covered the ceiling. On a small stage at the back of the room was a plastic palm tree wrapped with a string of lights. Nolan pulled out a stool and sat down at the bar. The bartender was an older woman with penciled eyebrows. She slapped a cardboard coaster in front of Nolan and said, "I got Anchor Steam. Two-dollar special tonight."

There were two others, a man and a woman, at the bar drinking schooners, and Nolan nodded and said, "Sure." They all stared up at the television. The Mariners were up by two, but Oakland sent up their best hitter, and soon the game was tied.

The bartender stood talking to the woman at the end of the bar. She had a smoker's mouth, and when she laughed it sounded like she'd swallowed something with claws. She stepped outside to have a cigarette, told them to shout if they needed anything. The man sitting two stools down from Nolan still slicked back his hair like it was 1957. His face was pockmarked. His shirtsleeves, rolled. He pulled a pack of cigarettes from his front pocket, snapped open the lid and closed it again. "Still weird to not be able to smoke in bars," he said to Nolan. He looked back up at the TV. The As scored again. "Crap," he said. "There goes that."

Nolan didn't know what he had expected. You couldn't go back in time. You couldn't really imagine, and why did he want to when his mother was all right now, when Wilkes was dead, when Nolan didn't have a single memory of any of it.

The man with the slicked-back hair wanted to buy a shot for Nolan and the woman at the end of the bar.

"OK," the woman said. "Why not. Make mine a raspberry kamikaze."

"Maureen," the bartender said. "You better not be driving home tonight."

"You know I never drive on Fridays," Maureen said. She tossed back the shot and wiped her mouth. She had red, runny eyes and the look of a professional drinker. She thanked the man but didn't get too close. She leaned over to touch the bartender's arm. "Call me a cab, will you? I might as well go home."

The bartender went around to the other side of the bar and put her arm around Maureen's shoulders and squeezed. She apologized for there not being more men around. "Next week we got karaoke. You come back then, honey. We'll fix you up good."

When the taxi arrived, Maureen stumbled out the propped-open door in her red cowboy boots, and the three of them watched her get into the cab. The bartender picked up her empty glass and plunged it into the suds behind the bar.

"You been working here long?" Nolan asked.

"Too long," she said.

"How long is that?"

"Almost six years now." She slapped a rag across the bar and turned around to glance up at the clock.

Nolan tried to picture the place as his mother had known it, full of customers, someone playing guitar up on stage. "One more for the road?" he asked the man. He felt obligated to buy a round.

"Sure," the man said. "What the hell."

The bartender poured them both another whisky, and Nolan paid. He couldn't feel the alcohol yet. His stomach was too full of steak, and he couldn't get comfortable on the padded stool. He asked for a glass of water, ate another handful of peanuts from the greasy bowl in front of him.

The man looked at Nolan as he tipped back the shot. "Thank you," he said, and then he sipped his unfinished beer. He played with the top of the cigarette pack, and his fingernails were long and yellowed and dirty, and everything in the bar seemed dirty too, and the bartender started to cough and pulled a balled-up tissue from her pocket and spat into it.

Nolan pushed himself back from the counter. "Thanks," he said to the bartender. "Take it easy," he said to the man and walked out into the cool night. If he got to sleep soon, he could get up early and make it downtown to get one of the better jobs. If that didn't work, he could sign up at a temp agency. He'd done that before.

Outside, he walked to the lot next to the motel, and Sigrid's car was gone. He went into the motel office and asked the man behind the counter about it, and the man said, "Didn't you see the sign? You can't park here if you're not a guest."

Nolan stepped under the awning of the tavern and took out his phone to call Sigrid. He'd have to wake her, and it would be like he was in high school again and in trouble, calling her because he'd wrecked the car or run out of gas or was too drunk to drive. There'd be a ticket he couldn't pay, his mother's car stuck at the impound lot.

A bus rolled down the street but didn't stop. He had probably missed the last one.

Just then, the man with the slicked-back hair left the bar. He walked like he had once been a much larger man and had lost a lot of weight.

"You all right, son?"

"Car got towed."

"Where you headed?"

"It's OK. I can walk."

"Come on. I'll give you a lift."

Nolan followed him down the street to his rusted Civic. The man said, "Just give me a sec to move some crap out of the front. Hell of a night, huh?"

There was a clear sky and a full, perfect moon. A car full of kids drove by and a long-haired girl stuck her head out the window and shouted something unintelligible.

"Somebody's having a good time," the man said. He looked up at the moon. "That kind of night. Crazies gonna come out."

Nolan tried the door, and the man said, "Sorry. Door's broken. Here, let me." He wiggled the handle until the door opened, threw a shaving kit and a stack of papers into the back and brushed some garbage onto the floor. "Hop in," he said.

The car smelled of fast food and the man's sweat. A suit was draped over a mound of laundry in the backseat. Nolan rested his feet on wrappers and empty paper cups. A rosary hung from the mirror, and underneath it on the dash was a bobble-headed dachshund.

"Where can I drop you?"

Nolan told him. "But you don't have to take me the whole way."

"I've got nowhere I need to be."

Nolan tried to make small talk, but the man drove and didn't say a word, and when Nolan finally quieted, the man said, "What do you do for a living, son?"

"Nothing right now. I just moved here. Still looking."

This seemed to make the man more interested. "That why you're all alone tonight? Ain't got no friends?"

They weren't driving that fast, maybe forty tops. The man's fingernails were too long. They were thick and ragged, and he clenched the steering wheel a little too hard. The inside handle of the passenger door was crushed in. If something went wrong, Nolan would have to throw his body against it, try to jimmy it open.

The man turned on the radio and listened. Scientists prove precognition in animals. That's right, folks. Apparently, a parrot in Brazil has been able to predict the actions of its keeper.

He turned the volume down. "You hear about that black bear down in Ballard?"

"No. What happened to it?"

"Made its way up north a ways. Someone spotted it in Edmonds, but then nothing. Just up and disappeared."

The car felt too cramped. The man seemed nice enough, but Nolan had an uneasy feeling. "You know what," he said. "I kind of feel like walking. It's so nice out. You can just let me off here."

"That's a long way to hoof it." The man nodded at the rosary hanging from the mirror. "You got nothing to fear from me, son, if that's what you're worried about."

Nolan laughed uncomfortably. "I think I drank too much," he said, though he was feeling all right. "I don't want to throw up in your car. It will help to walk."

"You think this car ain't been puked on before?" Now the man laughed. "I could tell you stories. Boy, could I." He reached over and patted Nolan's knee, and Nolan inched closer to the door.

"Then there was that coyote over in Discovery Park. They had to close the park down and tranquilize it. Took it up to the Cascades, but some say they seen it back again. That's the way it is, a thing's always got to come back home. You hear about the deer?"

He was heading the right direction, but in a roundabout way, taking all the narrow side streets. No people were out walking, but lights were on in apartments and houses.

"You ever listen to this show?"

"No," Nolan lied.

"Good stuff, I tell you. If you like weird stories and all."

They pulled onto 50th toward the zoo and wove around Woodland Park, and Nolan slumped back against the seat. The streets were darker here, the park closed. *And later in the hour, we've got a treat for you. Helmar Reiter, deep-sea linguist, will talk to us about teaching dolphins the alphabet.* There was more traffic now. He was almost home. "Two more lights, then hang a right," he said.

"Right about here someplace, that's where they saw them. One was a buck, I heard. Run right across four lanes at nine in the morning, then crashed into the Starbucks." The man whistled. "Cops had to shoot him. The others, they're still around here somewhere. Imagine surviving that every goddamned day of your life."

They waited at the light. Nolan could finally feel the booze. The light lasted forever. The man's hands clenched the wheel. Nolan couldn't stop staring at them, and the man noticed. He smiled. "I got a couple of bottles back at the ranch. Just a little ways from here. Not far at all and real quiet. What do you say?"

Nolan pushed at the handle, threw his weight at the door to get it open, but it wouldn't budge.

"Take it easy," the man said, but Nolan kept pushing. The light turned green. The man sped forward and took the next street, pulling over, shifting into park. "I got it," he said. "Hold on. Hold on."

The man pulled himself out of the car and wiggled the door open from the outside. "Get out you want out so bad."

Nolan climbed out. The man stood waiting, but Nolan couldn't look at him, couldn't even open his mouth to thank him. He started walking up the street, and then he broke into a run. He ran all the way up the hill and over three blocks until he got to

Sigrid's condo and let himself in. In his room, the radio was still on, and he yanked the plug from the wall and got into bed without changing out of his clothes. The room was bright with the moon. He'd stay awake all night if he had to. He'd figure it out. Why he was so angry. Why even his own mother was braver than he was. She'd gotten over something more horrific than he'd ever know in his whole damn life. He wanted to know how this was. How this could be when he couldn't even name what it was he was running from, and whether it was Wilkes that had made him this way. Arvel Wilkes standing over his crib and stroking a hand over Nolan's forehead, marking him a quitter or a survivor, Nolan didn't know which.

Something Transcendent at the Heart

Alison Umminger

Someone has slept with someone in the workshop, which shouldn't matter, but does. It's the mid-90s and the winners are wafer-thin poets with ringed eyes and syringe-sharp turns of phrase. This is the era of waifs and prickly poems, and mostly when you go to workshop you feel exhausted, because you are not a terribly good writer, nor are you a ring-eyed waif, nor is it fun to be in a workshop where attention is on the waifs and their poems, which, admittedly, are better than yours. And waifs is probably reductive, because the act of teacher-student bang-bang has thrown the psychodynamics of everything off – the classroom, meetings outside the classroom, teachers who are married but part of the problem: He-who-trolls-the space as destructive as she-who-punishes-the-castoffs. You are twenty-four and figure this is the way things go, for writers, at any rate.

No one has cell phones and between workshops you wander the three blocks that constitute the heart of a town that you could only find on a map with guidance before driving seventeen hours from the East Coast to the middle of nowhere for a degree in creative writing. One terribly bad night, you throw a pair of black mary-jane pumps at a band showing pornographic images and collapse in the middle of the street in tears. You should probably be medicated, talking to someone, but somehow you survive, and a few years later at a different school, you become part of this problem, a self-righteous twenty-something who should be writing apology letters to the universe for her behavior, but mostly just pouts at parties. You think back on the decade largely as bad decisions and loud sing-a-longs to angry women dressed like children: *Go on... take everything.* Only you're not even sure what's been taken or what anyone even wants. You gain and lose the same seven pounds about seventy times, all your apartments are infested with some form of poison-resistant critter, a few guys are a little too-stalky, and in return, you leave a few truly bizarre and unwanted messages on answering machines to men you've met once and draft letters that you drop into mailboxes wishing they might turn into love. In the movies, they do. In life, they disappear and you wonder why you are so unprepared at making a life. You scan the sidewalks for change when you walk and think writing a novel will save you. Even though those who have published novels tell you it won't, you are sure they are wrong.

Twenty-five years later, when you remember these times you honestly wish you had wanted to do something a little more...*useful.* This is ironic since you spend a good part of your job trying to convince students that writing is...*useful,* or at the very least, bankable, the sort of straw that can be spun into student-loan payments and shared rent. You are married, a mom, and you teach writing, but you are a boring teacher. Mostly, your students seem like children, and you want to take away their phones and, mostly, you say things like, "after twenty pages, I still don't know what this story is really *about*" or "*I am sorry that you dislike what this person said, but I cannot kick him out of workshop for that. We cannot cancel people in real life because we don't like what they are saying.*" This last one reminds you not of workshop in the 1990s, but being a history major in the 1980s, where you studied African, Latin American, and European history, and it seemed well understood that *cancelling* was a late-stop on a dark route you didn't want to follow.

Now your students are mad about *everything*, and *everything* feels like a cross between things that are truly appalling and things that don't matter at all, and you wonder when language, like outrage, reverted to broad strokes and volumetrics.

During your first year of graduate school you became friends with one of the cast-offs, a poet who could have been your "cool aunt," who showed up at your apartment unannounced with gifts like a walrus-hide covered journal, all so you would sit patiently and make tea as she mourned the end of a messy affair. Once a week, you would sit with this woman, and the waifs, and the professor, and some posturing guys, and everyone would pretend that none of these things happened outside the classroom, and mostly you would wish you had gone to a different school. At the same time, it was all new and sordid and fascinating. Until then, affairs were things people only had on television, with presidents, publicly shamed and ruined for life. Here, they were like Tic Tacs. You admired this women's work and liked her well enough, but knowing every part of her story made you feel complicit. Plus, she had a hot husband and the man for whom she pined looked, to you, like a smug frog. At the same time, you submitted poems and papers like offerings to the men who ran the classes. You wanted so very badly to be noticed.

Joan Collins once famously said that being beautiful was like being born rich and spending your life slowly going broke. At best, you were once middle-income, and as fifty looms close, you are down to your last five bucks. Your students will tell you that it's not *about* beauty, but that's because they are still beautiful, or at the very least, young. You now teach the books of writers who were your friends, and many who weren't, but who-knew-someone-who-knew someone. Recently, you taught Junot Diaz, a few months after you left social media and entered a classroom not truly prepared for the crossed-arms, *knowing what we know about this man, etc., etc.,* and all you can think is that he was raped as a child and that kissing someone at a reading does not feel like an unpardonable crime, and the gap between how you read a story and how they read a story widens like an earthquake in a '70's B-movie—one wrong word and you'll be the next to fall in. You ask not to teach fiction, not to teach contemporary literature, and even when teaching Ralph Waldo Emerson you find yourself trying to explain that he probably did not experience himself as "so privileged" because today is not yesterday is not two hundred years ago. He believed that at the center of each human was something transcendent. One of them says, *I don't believe in nature,* and they mean trees, not human, and you walk around thinking *four legs good, two legs better.*

A few weeks ago, you got news that the woman who had given you the walrus-hide journal had passed, and you remembered how beautifully she wrote, and how you grew to dread the ring on your call-box where she announced she was in the lobby, ready to lament the pointlessness of her love. Would that we could all go back and undo the past, shower our younger selves with the love and attention and base-line human kindness that seemed such a scarce commodity, doled out like puppy-treats in workshop settings.

A final anecdote: your most handsome teacher, too young for the slick machinations of advanced seduction, was still no friend of women. He returned one of your first-drafts with a page of single-spaced slice-and-dice stapled to the top. There was no way you could have separated the cruel from the true, and while the comments and story are lost to forgetting, you do remember the next week sitting in a circle of people and having him look at you and ask, *Did you get my comments?* You nodded. *Did they make you cry?*

You learned something in that moment, about the kind of person you didn't want to be.

Today, you fear you have become that person, inured to student tears and feelings and outrage, wondering why anyone thinks that the human condition can be outrun or outsmarted, too tired, even, to dream a utopia. You sort through your old earrings for a pair that your friend brought over one rainy afternoon, mint-green glass beads, inexpensive, but still part of your collection after decades of jewelry accumulation and culls. They looked antique, the day you were gifted them, as your friend lamented that her professor and seducer had moved on. You were tired of her too by then. She had a husband at home who hunted, who neither wrote nor read poems, who had no idea his wife was cheating on him. Some days, you felt complicit, maybe even jealous that she had something so precious to throw away.

About the Authors

Karen E. Bender is the author of the story collection *Refund*, which was a finalist for the National Book Award in fiction, shortlisted for the Frank O'Connor International Story Prize, and longlisted for the Story Prize; and *The New Order*, which was longlisted for the Story Prize. A new collection, *The Words of Dr. L*, is forthcoming from Counterpoint Press. Her novels are *Like Normal People*, a *Los Angeles Times* bestseller and *Washington Post* Best Book of the Year, and *A Town of Empty Rooms*. Her fiction has appeared in magazines including *The New Yorker, Granta, Ploughshares, Zoetrope, Story, The Yale Review, The Harvard Review, Guernica*, and others. Her work has been reprinted in *Best American Short Stories, Best American Mystery Stories, New Stories from the South: The Year's Best*, and has won three Pushcart prizes. Her work has been read by Joanne Woodward on Symphony Space's "Selected Shorts" series, and by Levar Burton on "Levar Burton Reads." She has received grants from the National Endowment for the Arts and the Rona Jaffe Foundation. She is Fiction Editor of the literary journal *Scoundrel Time*. Visit her at www.karenebender.com.

May-lee Chai is the author of eleven books, including her new short story collection, *Tomorrow in Shanghai;* the memoir *Hapa Girl*, a Kiriyama Prize Notable Book; her original translation from Chinese to English of the 1934 *Autobiography of Ba Jin;* and *Useful Phrases for Immigrants: Stories,* winner of a 2019 American Book Award. Her prize-winning short prose has been published widely, including in the *New England Review, Paris Review Online, Missouri Review, Seventeen, Crab Orchard Review, The Rumpus, ZYZZYVA,*

San Francisco Chronicle, and *Los Angeles Times*. The recipient of an NEA fellowship in prose, Chai is an associate professor in the Creative Writing Department at San Francisco State University.

Elizabeth Crane is the author of two novels and four collections of short stories, most recently the novel *The History of Great Things* and the story collection *Turf.* She is a recipient of the Chicago Public Library 21st Century Award. Her work has been featured on NPR's Selected Shorts and adapted for the stage by Chicago's Steppenwolf Theater. Her debut novel, *We Only Know So Much*, has been adapted for film. She teaches in the UCR-Palm Desert low-residency MFA program. A memoir, *This Story Will Change*, will be out in 2022 from Counterpoint Press.

Rebecca Entel's novel, *Fingerprints of Previous Owners*, was published by Unnamed Press in 2017. Her short stories and essays have been published in such journals as *Catapult, Guernica, Hobart, Cleaver, Jellyfish Review, Joyland, Literary Hub*, and *Electric Literature*. She is Professor of English and Creative Writing at Cornell College, where she teaches courses in creative writing, 19th-century U.S. literature, African-American literature, Caribbean literature, and the literature of social justice, and is the Robert P. Dana Director of the Center for the Literary Arts. She mentors in PEN America's Prison Writing Program and has taught fiction workshops for *Catapult.* A graduate of the University of Pennsylvania and the University of Wisconsin, she currently lives in Iowa City.

Gina Frangello's fifth book, the memoir *Blow Your House Down: A Story of Family, Feminism, and Treason* (Counterpoint), has been selected as a *New York Times* Editor's Choice and received starred reviews in *Publishers Weekly, Library Journal*, and *BookPage*. She is also the author of four books of fiction, including *A Life in Men*

(Algonquin), which is currently under development by Charlize Theron's production company, Denver & Delilah, and *Every Kind of Wanting* (Counterpoint), which was included on several "best of" lists for 2016, including *Chicago Magazine*'s and *The Chicago Review of Books'*. Now the Creative Nonfiction Editor at the *Los Angeles Review of Books*, Gina brings more than two decades of experience as an editor, having founded both the independent press Other Voices Books and the fiction section of the popular online literary community The Nervous Breakdown. She has also served as the Sunday editor for The Rumpus, and as the faculty editor for both *TriQuarterly* Online and *The Coachella Review*. Her short fiction, essays, book reviews, and journalism have been published in such venues as Salon, the LA Times, Ploughshares, the Boston Globe, BuzzFeed, Dame, and in many other magazines and anthologies, as well as having a column on the Psychology Today blog. She runs Circe Consulting, a full-service company for writers, with the writer Emily Rapp Black, and can be found at www.ginafrangello.org.

Joan Frank's most recent novel is *The Outlook for Earthlings.* Other recent books are *Where You're All Going: Four Novellas* (Gold Medal, 2021 Independent Publisher Book Awards; Mary McCarthy Prize in Short Fiction), published by Sarabande Books, and *Try to Get Lost: Essays on Travel and Place* (River Teeth Literary Nonfiction Prize). Joan's 2017 novel, *All the News I Need*, won the Juniper Prize for the Novel. Her essay collection, *Because You Have To: A Writing Life*, won the ForeWord Reviews Silver Book of the Year Award. Her past honors include the Richard Sullivan Prize, Dana Award, Iowa Writing Award, and notable others. Joan has received grants from the Barbara Deming Memorial Fund, Ludwig Vogelstein Foundation, and Sonoma Arts Council and has been nominated twice for the Northern California Book Award in Fiction. She has taught creative writing at San

Francisco State University and reviews literary fiction and nonfiction for *The Washington Post* and *Boston Globe*. She lives in Northern California.

Melissa Fraterrigo is the author of two books, *Glory Days* (University of Nebraska Press, 2017), which was named one of "The Best Fiction Books of 2017" by the *Chicago Review of Books*, as well as the short story collection *The Longest Pregnancy* (Livingston Press, 2006). Her fiction and nonfiction have appeared in more than forty literary journals and anthologies, among them *storySouth, Shenandoah, Notre Dame Review,* and *The Millions.* She is the founder of the Lafayette Writers' Studio in Lafayette, Indiana, where she teaches classes on the art and craft of writing.

Lynn Freed's books include seven novels, a collection of stories, and two collections of essays. Her short fiction and essays have appeared in *Harper's, The New Yorker* and *The Atlantic Monthly*, among numerous others. She is the recipient of the inaugural Katherine Anne Porter Award from the American Academy of Arts and Letters, two O. Henry Awards for fiction, and has received fellowships and grants from the National Endowment for the Arts and The Guggenheim Foundation, among others. Having grown up in South Africa, she came to the U.S. as a graduate student at Columbia University, where she received an MA and PhD in English Literature. She is Professor Emerita of English at the University of California, Davis, and lives in Northern California.

Amina Gautier is the author of three short story collections: *At-Risk, Now We Will Be Happy,* and *The Loss of All Lost Things. At-Risk* was awarded the Flannery O'Connor Award; *Now We Will Be Happy* was awarded the Prairie Schooner Book Prize in Fiction; *The Loss of All Lost Things* was awarded the Elixir Press Award in

Fiction. Gautier has been the recipient of fellowships and grants from the American Antiquarian Society, the Camargo Foundation, the Chateau de Lavigny, Dora Maar House/Brown Foundation, Kimmel Harding Nelson Center, MacDowell Colony, Ragdale, Vermont Studio Center, and the Woodrow Wilson Foundation. More than one hundred and thirty of her stories have been published, appearing in *Agni, Boston Review, Callaloo, Cincinnati Review, Glimmer Train, Greensboro Review, Gulf Coast, Joyland, Kenyon Review, Latino Book Review, Mississippi Review, New Flash Fiction Review, Quarterly West, Southern Review*, and *Triquarterly*, among other places. She is the recipient of the Blackwell Prize, Eric Hoffer Legacy Fiction Award, the Phillis Wheatley Book Award in Fiction, the International Latino Book Award, and the Chicago Public Library Foundation's 21st Century Award. For her body of work she has received the PEN/Malamud Award for Excellence in the Short Story. She teaches in the MFA program at the University of Miami where she is an Associate Professor of English and the Gabelli Senior Scholar.

Cris Mazza's most recent novel is *Yet to Come* (BlazeVox Books). Mazza has eighteen other titles of fiction and literary nonfiction including *Charlatan: New and Selected Stories*, chronicling twenty years of short-fiction publications; *Something Wrong With Her*, a real-time memoir; her first novel *How to Leave a Country*, which won the PEN/Nelson Algren Award for book-length fiction; and the critically acclaimed *Is It Sexual Harassment Yet?* In the mid-90s Mazza edited the groundbreaking *ChickLit* anthologies. She is a native of Southern California and is a professor in and director of the Program for Writers at the University of Illinois at Chicago.

Roberta Montgomery is a former editor at *The Atlantic* and wrote and produced many television game shows including "Liars," "Family Feud," and, "The Legends of the Hidden Temple."

Her short fiction has appeared in small magazines including *Chicago Quarterly Review*. She was a finalist for the Bakeless Prize for her novel, *A Romantic Husband*.

Victoria Patterson's latest story collection, *The Secret Habit of Sorrow*, was published in 2018. The critic Michael Schaub wrote: "There's not a story in the book that's less than great; it's a stunningly beautiful collection by a writer working at the top of her game." Her novel *The Little Brother*, which *Vanity Fair* called "a brutal, deeply empathetic, and emotionally wrenching examination of American male privilege and rape culture," was published in 2015. She is also the author of the novels *The Peerless Four* and *This Vacant Paradise*, a 2011 *New York Times Book Review* Editors' Choice. Her story collection, *Drift*, was a finalist for the California Book Award and the Story Prize and was selected as one of the best books of 2009 by the *San Francisco Chronicle*. She lives in South Pasadena, California with her family. She is an affiliate faculty member at Antioch University Los Angeles.

Jenny Shank's short story collection, *Mixed Company*, won the George Garrett Fiction Prize, and her novel, *The Ringer*, won the High Plains Book Award and was a finalist for the MPIBA Reading the West award. Her stories, essays, satire, and reviews have appeared in *The Atlantic, Washington Post, Los Angeles Times, The Guardian, McSweeney's Internet Tendency, The McSweeney's Book of Politics and Musicals, Dear McSweeney's: Two Decades of Letters to the Editor from Writers, Readers, and the Occasional Bewildered Consumer, Prairie Schooner, Alaska Quarterly Review, Michigan Quarterly Review, The Rumpus, The Toast, Poets & Writers Magazine* and *The Onion A.V. Club*. Her stories have been listed among the "Notable Essays of the Year" in the *Best American Essays* and have received "Special Mention" in the Pushcart Prize anthology. She has been a Mullin Scholar in Writing at the

University of Southern California and is on the faculty of the Lighthouse Writers Workshop and the Mile High MFA at Regis University in Denver. She has also published over a thousand book reviews and author interviews in such places as the *Minneapolis Star Tribune* and *Dallas Morning News*.

Christine Sneed's books are the novels *Paris, He Said* and *Little Known Facts*, and the story collections *Portraits of a Few of the People I've Made Cry* and *The Virginity of Famous Men*. Her fifth book, *Please Be Advised: A Novel in Memos*, is forthcoming from 7.13 Books. Her work has appeared in *The Best American Short Stories, O. Henry Prize Stories*, the *New York Times, O Magazine, New England Review, The Southern Review, Ploughshares, New Stories from the Midwest, Glimmer Train*, and many other periodicals. She has received the Grace Paley Prize in Short Fiction, the Society of Midland Authors Award, the Chicago Public Library's 21st Century Award, among other honors. She teaches for the MFA programs at Northwestern University and Regis University.

Rachel Swearingen is the author of *How to Walk on Water and Other Stories*, winner of the New American Press Fiction Prize and a *New York Times Book Review* "New & Noteworthy" selection. Her stories and essays have appeared in *Electric Lit, VICE, The Missouri Review, Kenyon Review, Off Assignment, American Short Fiction*, and elsewhere. A recipient of the Missouri Review Jeffrey E. Smith Editors' Prize in Fiction, a Rona Jaffe Foundation Writers' Award, and the Mississippi Review Prize in Fiction, she lives in Chicago and teaches in Cornell College's low-residency MFA program.

Alison Umminger is the author of the internationally published novel *American Girls*, and teaches English and creative writing at the University of West Georgia. Her stories, essays, and poems have appeared in *Quarterly West, Gulf Coast, Birmingham Poetry Review, Gawker,* among others, and she has won the Lawrence Foundation Prize for short fiction from *Prairie Schooner*. She was the fourth female president of *The Harvard Lampoon*, and is now (also) a retreat leader who recently completed her spiritual director studies at Loyola University-Chicago. While the distance between monastery and Lampoon may seem vast—there are more similarities than one might think.

Acknowledgments

"Former Virgin" was previously published in the collection *Former Virgin* (Fiction Collective 2, 1997) and in *Charlatan: New and Selected Stories* (Spuyten Duyvil, 2021)

"How to Walk on Water" was previously published in *The Missouri Review* and in the collection *How to Walk on Water* (New American Press, 2020)

"Potpourri" was previously published in *Michigan Quarterly Review: Mixtape*, Distortions issue, 2021

"Preferences" was previously published in *Pindeldyboz*, 2009

"Slut Lullabies" was previously published in the collection *Slut Lullabies* (Emergency Press, 2010) and in *Water~Stone Review*

"Sunshine" was previously published in *Narrative Magazine* (2010), *The O. Henry Prize Stories 2011* and the anthology *Dark End of the Street* (Bloomsbury, 2010)

"The Elevator" was previously published in *Guernica* and in the collection *The New Order* (Counterpoint, 2018)

About Tortoise Books

Slow and steady wins in the end, even in publishing. Tortoise Books is dedicated to finding and promoting quality authors who haven't yet found a niche in the marketplace—writers producing memorable and engaging works that will stand the test of time.

Learn more at www.tortoisebooks.com, find us on Facebook, or follow us on Twitter: @TortoiseBooks.